# About the

Jake Ridge is the pseudonym of Colin R Parsons. He's a fiction author who writes in many genres, such as: fantasy, science fiction, supernatural and steampunk. He lives with his wife, Janice, in the Rhondda Valley in South Wales, UK. He's been writing for over two decades and has had lots of books published for children and adults. He loves his job as an author and couldn't think of anything else he'd rather do.

# By the same author

Spirit Jumper & Strange Happenings

# Killian Spooks Mysteries: Phantom Thief

To Judit
Another Magical Journey

Best Wishes

JRidge

# Jake Ridge

## Killian Spooks Mysteries:
## Phantom Thief

**Pegasus**

PEGASUS PAPERBACK

A CIP catalogue record for this title is
available from the British Library

ISBN-978 1 91090 361 2

*Pegasus is an imprint of
Pegasus Elliot MacKenzie Publishers Ltd.*
www.pegasuspublishers.com

First Published in 2021

**Pegasus
Sheraton House Castle Park
Cambridge CB3 0AX England**

Printed & Bound in Great Britain

# Dedication

This is for Jim Burgess, a true friend and dedicated reader.

# Acknowledgements

My family, Jan, for putting up with me for all my writing career. To Kris and Ryan, my sons, whose support has never wavered. To my army of readers, for without them, I wouldn't be doing this.

## Chapter 1
## Being Followed

Killian struggled with the beast as it wriggled and snarled. The wizard had managed to get a muzzle over its jaws and that was a job and a half. So now at least it couldn't bite either of them, but he had the next part to do and that wasn't going to be easy either.

'Hold it down, for fuck's sake,' Killian hissed, his voice straining.

'I'm trying, I'm trying,' Zoot said, and applied more pressure, the wolf growled a deep guttural purr as Killian Gripped its muzzle. 'Killian. You do realise that I've got paws, not hands. And please stop cussing at me,' he complained bitterly. The animal they were trying to capture squirmed and twisted with everything it had and it was all they could do to contain it. Its deep red eyes were piercing; its breath and fur stank to high heaven. It was so powerful that at any moment it was going to break away.

'We're losing it, change back, for God's sake, Zoot, and you'll be able to grip it easier,' Killian insisted, his mouth in a grimace.

'Okay, okay,' Zoot agreed and began to morph. he could hear his friend the shapeshifter's bones cracking and the twisting of muscle. Killian cringed and creased up his face at every pop and groan until it was over. Zoot was back in his monk-like state once again.

'Right, grab its legs before it pushes me over again.' Killian strained to speak. Once Zoot had secured the rear end of the animal then things got a lot easier.

Killian had more of a grip and when the wolf was locked-down, he whispered a spell, his mouth only moving slightly. The wolfhound seemed to calm and wasn't struggling any longer. It fell limp and its eyes slowly began to shut. Soon it transformed from the raging wolf that had possessed it, to a normal family pet. Killian and Zoot could finally let go. That was it. They'd done it. Both of them fell back on their haunches. Killian looked at his naked friend.

'I know,' Zoot acknowledged and disappeared for a few moments. He retrieved his robe, which he'd hidden in the churchyard, and quickly slipped it on. He returned before anyone noticed.

'Well, that was easy,' Killian said whilst blowing air through his lips.

'Yeah, right,' Zoot retorted.

'What's he doing now?' the strained voice of the priest called out, his lungs wheezing from the short, jog across the graveyard.

'Sleeping,' Killian said softly. 'It'll be fine now, Father,' he assured him.

'The evil spirit… gone and Rex is okay?' the old man asked.

'Yes, for good hopefully,' Killian added. The vicar looked more at ease and knelt at the dog's side. He gently cradled its head and stroked him fondly.

Zoot looked on in admiration at what Killian had just achieved. He nodded sympathetically towards the wizard.

'Who's your friend? And where did your dog go?' Father Wilson asked, puzzled.

'Oh, this is Zoot, Father. He's a —'

'Monk. I kind of got that,' Father Wilson grinned. 'Does he speak?'

'Yes, I do.' Zoot,' spoke up. 'Nice to meet you, Father Wilson.'

'Likewise,' Father Wilson responded. 'You didn't answer my question. Where did your dog go?'

'Oh, he went home. Always does when he's hungry. And Zoot just happened to be taking a late evening stroll,' Killian lied.

'Yes, a late evening stroll,' Zoot repeated and gave Killian a quick, wicked, glance.

'Okay, it's late and we've got to go, Father,' Killian chirped up. He looked into the clergyman's eyes for a moment or two. Then it dawned on the vicar.

'Oh, the money,' Father Wilson remembered, 'of course yes.' He slipped his hand in his robe and handed Killian an envelope.

'Thank you kindly. If you have any more problems, don't hesitate to call me, but things should be fine now,' Killian assured him as he walked away. Zoot followed behind. They left the churchyard and made their way to the pub.

'It was a great idea to use me as bait for that possessed dog to follow me,' Zoot said, the sarcasm dripping from every word.

'Stop complaining, you enjoyed it really,' Killian teased. 'Do you want a pint?' Killian asked with a raw smile. Zoot looked at him incredulously.

'You know I don't drink alcohol, Killian,' Zoot scolded.

'Oh, I know. I just love to see you tell me off. Here, have this.' Killian delved into the envelope

14

and handed him some cash. 'And don't snap it out of my hand.' Killian was giggling now.

'Oh, you're full of it tonight, aren't you? Funny guy,' Zoot said. 'Hey, that's too much, Killian,' he protested.

'It's what you deserve. You've worked like a dog tonight, you know,' Killian said and broke into a broad smile.

'Shut up, you idiot,' Zoot grinned.

'I honestly couldn't have done it without you.' Zoot could tell he was serious now. 'Do you want me to give you a lift home?' Killian suggested.

'What, have a ride on your crappy scooter again?'

'Hey, you'll hurt her feelings,' Killian said.

'No, thanks,' Zoot said. 'I'll use my transport, thank you very much. Bye,' Zoot added as he walked away. Killian made his way along the road to the pub where his bike was parked outside.

'Talk soon, bye,' Killian called out, but when he heard the flapping of wings and saw a bird take flight into the night sky, he grinned. *That's the power of being a shapeshifter, I suppose*, he thought. Killian envied his friends ability, but there again, being a wizard had its moments. He continued walking and had a warm feeling of relief from a job well done. The Square Inn pub was only a matter of a few hundred yards away. It was his favourite place. It was a warm, overcast evening; he didn't mind the stroll. He ran the scenario with the possessed dog over in his mind again and puffed out a mouthful of air. Those things could go either way, he pondered. He continued ambling along. *A quick pint and that's it, drive home.*

It was quiet for a Wednesday and being ten-thirty, most of the inhabitants of Windy Vale were at home watching telly, or in bed sleeping for work the next day. Killian stepped onto the road to cross over. There was a light evening mist coming in from the sea. The tarmac was damp and glistened from the glow of the streetlights. He'd only made it halfway across when he stopped. There was something not quite right.

He quietened his breathing and listened. What was it? He felt as though someone was watching him from the shadows somewhere. This wasn't good. The next thing to happen was one of the streetlights started to flicker and a brisk wind whipped up from nothing. Killian darted his eyes from left to right.

'Zoot, is that you?' he called out, knowing that it couldn't be his friend. Zoot had long gone and was probably home by now. Killian's stomach tightened, as his hands began to tingle. This was serious. When his wizard's intuition was heightened, then normally something was wrong.

This wasn't a mugger or someone human watching him; no, this was something with magical or supernatural energy. He dipped into his pocket for his silver pen. Once this was touched, it would turn into his wand. He pulled it out and held it up, the tip sparking and spitting with magical energy. This made him feel less vulnerable.

Killian's heart quickened and he could feel the sweat building under his arms and across his chest. His face glistened with more perspiration and his breathing sharpened. 'I know you're there,' he declared to the darkness. 'Come out and show yourself. If you want to confront me, that is, do it where I can see you. Come on, face me and stop cowering in the shadows,' Killian insisted. He was beginning to get annoyed. He waited for whatever was there, but he realised that it wasn't going to show itself. Not yet, anyway.

'I'm fucking waiting,' Killian pressed, the anger building. He was trembling and that only happened when evil was near. He swallowed hard, his mouth, dry. He flicked his gaze to the left when he sensed movement. And with that, a darkened figure approached, as quick and as fluid as smoke. Killian's eyes were wide and he was tensed ready for a battle, but with what?

17

He stepped back and held his wand out in front, the tip burning brightly. The darkened figure stood silent right in front of him. But Killian couldn't distinguish anything familiar about this being.

'Who are—' Killian was about to ask when suddenly an elderly gentleman walking his dog appeared out of nowhere. The attacker instantly dissolved in front of Killian's eyes and the warlock was alone in the middle of the road. Killian immediately put his wand back in his pocket.

The old man approached and looked at Killian with suspicion.

'Good evening.' Killian spoke softly with a slight tremble and nodded. The man grunted something and the dog looked up and began yapping. The energy Killian felt had diminished and the tingling in his fingers had ceased. The dog looked confused as if it saw something but didn't believe its own eyes. It carried on growling and barking profusely — tugging at its lead, jerking its owner's arm.

'Slow down, Jasper, you mad thing,' the old man grumbled and tugged at the leash. He soon shuffled off into a garden further along the road, the pensioner moving as quickly as he could to his house. Killian had scared him.

The warlock stood there in a bath of sweat, still trembling slightly, but the danger had gone; the tense atmosphere, dissolved.

'What the fuck was that all about?' he whispered, the anger still inside. He slowed his breathing and relaxed. 'I don't like this. I don't like this at all,' he repeated. The wind had diminished. The streetlight stopped flickering and everything went back to normal. He waited a little longer until a car came up the road and he stepped onto the pavement. He changed his mind about visiting the pub. 'Sod it; I'm going to have a whisky back at my place. Killian rode a powder-blue Vespa and when he parked it up — rendered it invisible so that no one would think to steal it. He loved his scooter and cast a spell, which revealed it by the side of a dumpster where no one would look.

He rode home and parked his motorbike in its usual spot under the stairs. He then made straight for his apartment. When he got to the top of the stairs, he noticed a parcel leaning against the doorframe. Attached was a small envelope. He recognised the handwriting straightaway. It was Penny's, his work colleague and girlfriend.

He found his keys, then opened the door and picked up the parcel as he went. He closed the door behind him and walked through his office into his apartment. He dropped the parcel on the coffee table and quickly made for his liquor cabinet, after hanging up his jacket. He sat on the sofa and swallowed back a double whisky; the hot liquid bit hard in the back of his throat. 'I need to be on my guard from now on. Whatever that was, it will come back,' he reasoned. He hated it when he didn't know what he was up against. He tried to forget about it for now and turned his attention to the package. He eased back into the worn-out, leather sofa and peeled back the top of the letter. It read:

*Another weird case for you, sweetie. See you later, my sexy wizard.*

Killian giggled to himself. Then he turned to the package. He knew that it was a file from police headquarters before he ripped off the seal. Killian smiled again when he pictured Penny writing the note. He set the folder down on the table, spread it open and peered at the first page.

'Mmmm, reports of people being pickpocketed, but there is no recorded evidence on CCTV. An invisible thief, eh? And, it's all happening in the same area too,' he mumbled. 'I'll have to check this out in the morning.' Shit, he remembered that he had to pay Glyn, his landlord, the rent. He smiled when he conjured Glyn's face. That guy was always teasing him and he loved that about the old man. Things had been a bit lean lately, but he had the money now. He tossed the file on the coffee table and poured himself another glass of whisky, took a sip and dreamily closed his eyes as it swilled around in his mouth and he swallowed. He slumped back on the sofa and made himself comfortable. One more drink and he'd make his way to bed…

# Chapter 2
## Vivid

Killian could feel someone or something following him. It wasn't so much that he could hear anything or see a glimpse of a figure; it was just that familiar sense of knowing there was a presence. It was so difficult to see anything anyway. It was so depressingly dark here, blacker than black. He moved along the ground slowly and steadily. It was uneven and difficult to walk on without tripping here and there.

He needed light so he dipped in his pocket for the wand. He stopped... it wasn't there. Where the fuck was it? Killian tried to think when he'd held it last, but the memory didn't come. Where the fuck was he, and what was going on? This whole thing felt so weird. He tried to pick up the pace but it was difficult when everywhere was dense black.

Strangely, all he could hear was his breathing. Wherever this place was, it was as still as the grave. There was no breeze or rustling of trees. There wasn't even any birdsong or barking dogs. Killian stopped. He could still feel the presence somewhere in all that black. He was scared and why wouldn't he be? There was something following him and without his wand how was he meant to defend himself? He swallowed hard and the dryness in his throat made him hack at the back of his throat, which echoed. He must be in a tunnel or cave. Again, he questioned himself, how did he get here? He was panting and his body felt so tired. This wasn't good.

*Come on Killian think*, he told himself. You're a wizard. *You don't need your wand to fight back; you've got plenty of magic inside.* With that thought, he felt stronger. He began to move again with purpose. A little further along he saw light, but he had to be careful. There could be anything between him and the way out. His excitement and confidence began to lift. It would be a more level playing field once he was out in the open. He'd never been so exhilarated to get to a source of light in his life. The illumination wasn't a brilliant white; it was more of a pale-yellow glow, which seemed to pull at him like a powerful magnet.

He could still feel the stalker, not far behind but edging closer. But Killian began to feel stronger somehow — his wizard's magical force filling his body. His breathing, though, became more urgent the closer he got to the light.

23

He was sucking at the air with urgency as if gasping for oxygen, like an asthmatic. Whatever was behind was evil and was clawing at his lungs. The warlock pressed on. He knew it would only be a matter of seconds before he was out of there. He could feel a smile lift his tired face. Finally, he was outside in the open and didn't feel scared any more.

The depressing atmosphere inside the cave was behind him and he breathed freely. He quickly made his way to an open, flat area of ground. He stopped and turned around. He craned his neck and could see shapes in the background. They appeared as mountains but weren't somehow. This was all too strange. The weak light came from way in the distance.

Killian stood and waited to see whatever it was that was going to reveal itself. Soon a cooling wind whipped across his damp face, a pleasant and comforting friend. Killian focused his attention on the thick, black opening. Keeping an eye on the hole in the mountain, he raised his hands and cupped them together. He mouthed something and concentrated. Soon a glow appeared in the centre of his palms. The glow evolved into brighter, whiter energy. With his hands, he rolled and moulded it into a powerful ball of light. The brilliance illuminated his darkened face. He could sense the evil force getting closer and closer until suddenly, a figure appeared at the mouth of the cave.

'Hold it right there, demon,' Killian called out. The silhouette, though, kept on coming. 'I said stop. Are you fucking deaf?' Killian shrieked. It did stop when it was standing directly opposite him on the open ground. There was only the slight shimmer of a breeze and the crackle of energy from the wizard's hands. 'Who are you and what do you want with me?' Killian demanded. But the dark figure said nothing and stayed dormant. 'Answer me, evil one,' Killian bellowed, but it didn't move or speak. Killian separated his hands, which made the energy ball split in two. He stood with his hands upturned and pointed directly at the strange figure. Still, the apparition watched him, cool and silent, as if nothing phased it.

Killian took a moment to examine his enemy. It was tall, about six-foot-six at least. There wasn't much definition to work with. It was in kind of a black robe and its overall shape was of a human, but Killian knew that it was a demon of some sort. 'Are you going to answer me or do I have to kill you? Right here, right now!' Killian demanded.

There was a slight movement in the black mass and Killian tensed in readiness. Then sounds came from it.

'I am waiting for you, Killian Spooks.' It finally spoke. Its low tone made the ground vibrate under Killian's feet and he shuddered. This thing was more powerful than he had thought.

'Waiting for me?' Killian spoke back. His voice felt weak as the words fell from his mouth. 'Where is this place and what am I doing here?' Killian questioned with more determination.

'It's your time to pay,' the voice rumbled.

'Pay? Pay, for what? I don't even remember having a meal with you,' Killian joked. 'I don't owe you anything, demon,' he rasped.

'I'll be waiting,' the voice answered simply and with that made a lunge towards the wizard. Killian instinctively aimed and fired the energy balls at the advancing figure. The fiery spheres exploded on impact, turning the black mass into a large fireball. But it kept on coming with two flaming, hands reaching out for Killian's throat.

The sorcerer stumbled backwards as the beast gripped around his neck. He fell to the ground, the weight of the demon heavy on his body. He stared into two blood-red eyes and a mouthful of needle-sharp teeth. Killian screamed as he struggled and tried to hold the devil back. It picked him up by the throat and held him on the edge of a cliff.

'Wh-at is it th-at I owe you, de-mon?' Killian tried to choke out the words. He twisted his neck to see a deep crater below with wild, burning flames at its base.

'*Die*!' the demon screeched. Then it let go and he fell, down, down, down…

Killian's body was stiff as a stick. His eyes burst open, the fear clear in his mind. He tried to focus on where he was. It was early morning and twilight spilt in from partly opened curtains. He was in his room, in bed. He was sweating profusely and puffing like an ancient diesel train at top speed. His tee-shirt and shorts were soaked in perspiration.

'Oh shit… Jesus!' Killian retorted with an open mouth. It was a nightmare. Killian never normally suffered from those. The sheets were damp and he could feel a puddle of sweat in the middle of his chest. His brown, floppy hair was pasted to his scalp. Killian raised his hands and they were trembling, so he clenched them into fists. He groaned as he pushed himself into a sitting position and rested his back on the headboard. It was cool to the touch and comfortable.

His muscles were still stiff and his shoulders ached from the previous night's activities. He waited until he'd calmed down and craned his neck. 'What the fuck was that all about?' He looked at the clock; it was two-thirty in the morning. Killian's breathing was still higher than

27

normal when he got up and went to the bathroom for a pee. After he'd finished washing his hands, he leant on the washbasin and stared into the mirror. There were droplets of perspiration streaming down his forehead. He looked at his ghostly reflection for a while in the darkened room, the images from the dream still in his head. His body ached so much, and his head was drumming.

'That's twice it's visited me now,' Killian whispered to his image in the mirror. What did this demon want with him, he pondered? 'What do I owe it? What does it expect me to pay back?' he said and ground his teeth. Killian hated it when he didn't have the answers. 'Shit,' he hissed shaking his fist on the rim of the basin in temper. He caught his hand and tried to shake away the pain.

He was too tired to try and figure it out there and then. He was thirsty, but grabbed a couple of painkillers from the cabinet before he went any further. On the way back to his bed, he grabbed a bottle of ice-cold water from the fridge, the light from the open door whitening his tanned features. He tossed the tablets into his mouth and took a few hard gulps. He placed the bottle back inside and the room darkened again when he swung the door shut.

It was quiet and humid in his bedroom, the heat still lingering from the hot day they'd just endured. There was a luminous glow through the curtains. Killian realised that a strawberry moon was filtering in from outside. He sat on the bed and lay on top of the sheets. The material was damp and stuck uncomfortably to his back.

The dream, if it was one, was really vivid, too vivid. He kept on seeing its eyes in amongst all those flames. Killian tried to shut his mind from the image. He rolled over to his side and for the first time reached out for Penny. They'd only slept together a couple of times, but it seemed that the other side of the bed was hers now. He imagined her there and could feel his excitement. Her curvy figure pressed against the bedsheet. Her swathe of black hair tangled over the pillow. And the slow rise and fall of her breathing as she slept. He could almost smell her perfume and feel the warmth of her body. He gently stroked the duvet cover and imagined her smooth, skin under his fingertips. It took a while for him to drop back off to sleep. But when he did, it was Penny he thought about and not the nightmare. He drifted away with Penny in his arms and a smile on his face.

# Chapter 3
## The Calling

Killian woke later that morning and took a shower. He was still a little stiff from the previous night's activities — wrestling with the 'devil dog'. These small cases weren't big payers but, when things were lean, moneywise, they kept the wolves from the door

Killian took a stretch and assumed Zoot was feeling the same way, but his friend always seemed to heal quickly; but Killian also knew that his friend owned a special box that held a stone with healing powers. Killian also hadn't slept well. His head was full of the incident that happened on the road outside the pub and the scary dream he'd had. It had felt familiar and he assumed the demon was haunting him. He wracked his brains but couldn't figure out why he was being targeted.

Killian knew that he had enemies. You can't be a wizard and fight evil opponents without picking up an enemy or two. Besides everything else, he was also carrying a slight hangover too. He peered at the empty whisky bottle on the drainer and the glass tumbler discarded on the coffee table. He shook his head.

'I need to slow down on that stuff,' he said and made a coffee. He then remembered the file and picked it up off the coffee table. He walked into his office and flopped the folder on his desk. There were victim statements to read, but he didn't bother with them at this point. He ran his eyes over the details of the thefts and realised that they were all taking place at the Windy Vale train station. That's where he needed to start. It was a petty crime but it was the way in which the crimes were taking place that baffled the police. So, it was worth checking out and more importantly, there was money at the end of it.

He looked at the time and sighed. The day was already going too quickly. He'd slept in and so morning was soon the beginnings of early afternoon. He hadn't eaten breakfast and so decided to buy lunch at the Square Inn, his favourite haunt. Killian left his bike at home and walked to the pub. It was a nice, warm day again and he decided he needed the exercise. It wouldn't hurt to clear his head. The days were long and hot and he tried to remember when it had rained last. He'd also promised himself that he wasn't going to drink any more that day. So, when he got there, he ordered the lunch special and added a glass of ice water, instead of his usual pint of Cambrian beer. After he'd eaten his ham, egg and chips, he decided that before he went to the station, he'd take a walk back to the road where he'd encountered the strange experience the night before. He took a deep breath before he approached the spot, but didn't need to. It had a different feel to the night before and wasn't anywhere near as scary.

It was two o'clock in the afternoon and the road was quite busy.

He stood for a while as close as he could to the same place. The traffic was buzzing so he couldn't stand in the road; that would look ridiculous in the middle of the afternoon anyway. Killian didn't get any strange sensations at all — no trace of anything supernatural. He was beginning to doubt if it had ever happened and walked further along towards the church. That all looked calm enough too. He even saw Father Wilson walking his sheepdog around the grounds. The dog looked happy enough, chasing a ball that the priest had tossed for him. Killian didn't get any bad vibes from the churchyard either and realised that the evil spirit that had possessed the dog must have gone. Was it connected or was he getting paranoid?

'Good,' Killian said and shrugged it off. Satisfied, he moved on to his next destination — the train station. The station was towards the bottom end of Windy Vale. It was a modern building with a large car park. Just beyond it was a supermarket, which Killian thought was a great place to put one. People heading for the train in the mornings could grab lunch on the way, and passengers disembarking could drop in for essentials.

As he approached, he saw that there was a lot of hustling and bustling on the platform. It was the two-thirty p.m. train from Lewis Ville and friends were eager to meet in coffee shops and tourists to visit the castle. Killian gave a shudder when he remembered the case he'd done inside the castle grounds, but that was done. The warlock climbed the steps to the bridge that overhung the track. He leaned over and scrutinised the crowds of people. There was so much going on that it was really difficult to pinpoint anything. He was so happy that he didn't live in the city. There were too many people and too many vehicles. He liked the calm of Windy Vale. He grabbed an apple from his pocket and started munching away. He was getting a bit bored as he finished his fruit and tossed the core in a bin. He took one more look around for luck.

He swept his eyes from left to right, combing the area with his sight and magical powers. He breathed out as the oil and fumes from the engine seeped into his nostrils. There was nothing happening. Hold on! What was that? Killian stood poised.

He concentrated on a tall man in a suit who was just buying a newspaper from a vendor, nothing strange in that. The guy was leaning towards the stallholder with his wallet open and handing him the money for the paper. Meanwhile, as Killian looked on — and unbeknown to other passers-by — he could see the flap at the back of the guy's suit jacket suddenly lift up on its own.

Killian was intrigued and leaned further over the handrail and strained to see who was doing it. He could make out a mobile phone, which was sticking out of his back pocket. Then, mysteriously, it levitated into mid-air and disappeared in seconds. A smile lifted the wizard's face; he'd found the culprit. Killian whispered something under his breath and the spell revealed the figure of a young man. He looked like an ordinary teenager and Killian expected an ancient character from the sixteenth century at least. The thief must have felt something too because he immediately looked up, straight into Killian's eyes. Killian could tell that he was shocked because he broke the stare and immediately disappeared into the crowd.

'Great,' Killian grunted, 'why the hell didn't I hide?' He was about to make chase when something else also caught his eye. Another dark figure appeared at the end of the platform. It looked like a man but was too far away to know for sure. But what Killian did know was that this guy was also not of this world. Killian stood there, perfectly still at first, and then his hands began to tingle. It was the same feeling he'd had the previous evening. What did this evil thing want with him? He decided to abandon the pickpocket and follow the stranger. Killian quickly ran down the iron steps, weaving past the throng of commuters in his descent. He hurriedly scampered along the platform, which was fast emptying. By the time he'd got to the place where he'd seen the apparition, it was gone. But when the wizard looked through the gate in the direction of the street, he saw the figure again, moving towards the park.

He didn't waste any time and quickly followed his suspect. Windy Vale had an amazing park that stretched from the top end of the town to the bottom. But taking in the views was the last thing on his mind as he ran. He sprinted along the path that led deep into the heart of the wooded area of the park. He stopped and took a moment to catch his breath.

'Where are you? Where are you?' he repeated, probing the immediate vicinity with intense scrutiny. Then he spotted him again, moving along the winding path, up a hill towards the thick treeline. Still panting, the wizard made chase. He must have looked a sight. It was a rather hot day and he was dressed in trousers, shirt and boots. He sped along the ground like a greyhound, the sweat dripping down his face. Soon his shirt had damp patches under the arms and across the chest. Killian eventually made it to the top of the hill. He was straining to breathe and his mouth was so dry he could have swallowed an ocean. To top it off, he'd lost his suspect.

'Shit-shit-shit,' he cursed and let out a massive grunt. He leaned over, resting his hands on his knees, trying to get some oxygen into his lungs. He scanned the area for a while, but it was no use. Whoever it was had gone. 'Shit!' Killian scolded himself again through gritted teeth, but soon calmed. He needed a rest; his legs were like jelly. 'I need to lay off the booze and start doing some exercise,' he said, knowing it would never happen. He looked around for somewhere to sit.

He found a bench, sat down and closed his eyes. The temperature was at its peak and there wasn't a cloud in the sky. He leaned back and spread his arms along the top of the seat. He let out a long, winded sigh. Heart of hearts, he was devastated to lose his target, but he knew that that wasn't going to be the last encounter. Whoever is looking for me will return, Killian thought.

I'd better get back to the train station and see if I can find that young poltergeist again, he told himself. Things weren't working out too well at the moment. He was about to get up and walk away when he felt something.

His mouth dropped open, his eyes widened and he sat up straight. His tingly senses in his hands and stomach were electrically charged. Not only that, but he thought he'd heard something too. Killian concentrated, using all his awareness. These sensations he was feeling were the same as the night before... and the train station earlier. There it was again the voice he'd heard before — he was sure of it. The sound seemed to be coming from behind him. Killian immediately spun around and rested both hands on the top board of the bench. He studied the trees and bushes, but couldn't make anything out. The sun beat down on him and the lack of fluid made him feel light-headed. He swallowed hard but his mouth and throat were sticky with no saliva. He was on his own, thank God. He didn't need to endanger the public.

'Who are you?' he mumbled. 'Who's there?' he said in a commanding voice, getting more frustrated by the second. There was a sound, like someone shuffling about in the bushes. 'Come out and show yourself,' he demanded and grabbed his wand from his pocket; it crackled into life. Killian held it in front of him. All he could hear was the spit and crackle of the tip, smouldering. But besides that, only the gentle wind toying with branches and rustling the leaves. And a soft voice… echoes of someone calling him from way inside the treeline. This was a trap! It had to be, but he needed to investigate — it was pulling at him.

Killian looked around the wooded area of the park. Whoever had picked this place was playing a strategic game and knew they were on their own.

Okay, Killian, he told himself. Whoever this is, you have to be one step ahead. He got up from the bench and walked closer to the treeline. His stomach was doing cartwheels and his hand was trembling. He took a deep breath and stepped around the bench and headed for the trees. As he walked into the shade, he didn't know if he really wanted to find anything.

# Chapter 4
## Little Boy Lost

The light from his wand shone brightly in the dense undergrowth of trees and high grass. Even though it was a sunny day, inside there was shade and almost darkness in places. Killian wasn't only tingling with magical energy – he was also trembling with fear of the unknown. He'd already encountered this being a couple of times and it had got the better of him on each occasion. Something was happening here that he didn't have any control over. It was also very powerful and that frightened him even more. He stopped at an area that was free of twisted roots and loose branches. If he were attacked right there, at least it would be easier to manoeuvre and not trip on something. There was daylight here and when he looked up could see fragments of blue through the branches.

'Show yourself. Come on, man. This is getting a little tedious,' Killian called out nervously. 'You want me, then here I am. You just keep running away. Are you afraid of me?' He waited for something to happen, a reaction, but it didn't.

'What the fuck is going on here?' he ranted, his breath coming in laboured blasts and his temper stretched to the limit. 'I'm not playing your little game, guy,' Killian hissed. He moved further along. The grass beneath his feet was damp from being covered in the shade of the trees. The ground sloped in a long, sharp drop and was difficult to walk on. He moved cautiously but slipped on the wet ground landing on his backside and sliding halfway down the slope. 'Aaargh,' he cried out, until he dug in his heels and finally stopped. 'Fucking great,' he winced, feeling stupid. Luckily, he had kept his grip on the wand and managed to get back up on his feet. The back of his shirt and trousers were damp and his anger was just about bubbling under the surface.

Killian knew that he had to keep calm or he would be at a disadvantage. He reasserted himself and kept his wits about him and his eyes trained on anything that moved. He could hear the gentle flow of water in the background and the shrieks of a couple of crows, cawing and fighting in the trees. He would give anything to be up there taking his chances with them right now. Instead, he was down here...

He eventually came to a halt when the ground levelled off again. It was kind of like a small garden. Trees and dense greenery surrounded him and the thick, grassy carpet beneath his feet was almost flat, like a pool table. He held out his wand and peered at the other side of the open ground.

'This is nuts. Why have I been brought here?' He asked himself, having more questions and no answers. There was something unusual though, just a little further ahead of the space he was standing. He squinted through the mesh of foliage and felt that his sight was playing tricks on him and the reason for that was a kind of distortion, warping his vision. Killian squinted as if his eyes weren't seeing true, but something was blocking his view. It was as if there was a translucent panel or wall of energy that was obscuring his way. It appeared almost as if a summer haze was rippling before his eyes or reflecting like a mirror. But because it was cooler in there, too cool for a heat haze. He was transfixed on the image, as if hypnotised. Killian lifted his left hand and rubbed around his mouth and chin, which he always did when he was anxious.

What is this thing? He was getting more nervous by the second — this must be the source. The window just hovered there and now and then there was a slight ripple in the lens. It was the sudden movement that caught his interest; it gave a distortion to its surroundings. If you weren't looking for it, then you wouldn't have seen it.

Killian walked towards the phenomenon and stood within two metres of the magical picture frame. He set his wand in an arc to see where its boundaries ended. It seemed to stretch out to a three-metre diameter. Killian took a quick look around to make sure he wasn't being watched. There only seemed to be him and the object; it was surreal. He plucked up the courage to speak.

'Okay. So I'm here.' His voice sounded small and monotone in the dense surrounding. 'What is it you want?' he asked directly. He waited for an answer but nothing happened. Killian gave a heavy sigh and lowered his wand, the tip extinguishing immediately, but he kept a hold of it. He assumed that if this thing were going to hurt him, then it would have done so already. 'What do you want?' he snapped. He was getting frustrated. 'Fuck it. I need to touch this thing to find out what it's all about.' Reluctantly, he put his wand away, and it changed back into a silver pen and he slipped it into his pocket.

He decided to walk around the back and see what it looked like from the other side, and he did so. It was no different and only gave a view of where he'd just been. From what he could make out, it was circular and suspended about a metre from the ground. Killian took a quick look at its edge. It was so slim — like a razor blade — and it was impossible to make anything out at this angle. He wiped away a drip of snotty sweat from his nose with his hand and wiped it on his trousers. He walked to the front and looked hard. It still rippled every couple of seconds, like a phone signal, dipping in and out. Killian raised his hand, palm flat. He slowly got within touching distance. It was neither giving off heat nor cold.

'Why have you come here?' he yelled, his patience diminished. 'What do you want with me?' There was still no reply. Killian had come to the end of his tether. He didn't know what to do. Should he just go and leave this strange object? No, something was telling him that he had to touch it, to understand why it was there. He raked his fingers through his brown, wavy hair, his green eyes reflecting against the surface of the window. He reached out and gingerly, with his hand trembling, Killian inched his way closer and closer. His breathing became rapid and his heart pumped as if he'd just had a long run. He licked his lips and swallowed gulp after gulp. He could feel his hand trembling so much that he had to use his left hand to steady it. The object didn't give off heat, but Killian's face was a bathed in sweat. His finger was almost to the point of touching, his mouth wide open. As he leaned in, he stumbled slightly. He touched the surface before he was ready, but in that split-second he dropped something on the ground. Immediately after... everything went black.

The next moment he had the sensation of floating. He was weightless. How was that possible? Soon his feet touched down on a flat surface. Killian couldn't see anything. He couldn't hear anything. There was dampness to the air, which smelt like rotten wood or something dank and mouldy. He could still feel his outstretched arms and dropped them to his side. He stood just breathing and tried to make out where he was. It was like wearing a blindfold. What had he done? Where was he? Was he still in his world? If not, how was he going to get back? He must be inside the Dark World. His dream came flooding back from the early hours. For the first time in his life, he felt like a little boy lost from his mama. If he was on the other side — this was bad, very bad! He had to get back, right away. Memories, bad ones, floated through his mind.

It had been many hundreds of years since he'd set foot in here and he remembered that he had enemies here too. The reason he'd escaped in the first place was to find a better life for himself, on the other side, and he had. So who had brought him back? When he'd been part of this world, his job had been to help those poor, desperate people to get their souls back and send them on to their resting place. This world was a state of limbo for them. But the dark powers that resided in this dark place liked to manipulate, the weak and innocent. Oh fuck, why didn't he leave well alone and walk away from that fucking window? Perhaps it wasn't the dark world, but heart of hearts, he knew that it was. It had all the old feel of something that you'd rather forget.

'Think-think-think, Killian,' he mumbled. 'I need my wand for a start.' He quickly felt in his pocket and was relieved to find his wand was still there. A huge gasp left his throat and a smile filled his face. At least he had the means to defend himself. He urgently pulled it from his pocket and a stream of bright light lit the tip, with wisps of grey smoke lifting into the air. It made no difference though. All Killian could make out was the dense blackness. He stayed put for a while with the sound of the hiss and crackle of his wand. But he felt compelled to move forward, why he didn't know? He slowly began walking and ended up at the mouth of a giant cave. Killian stopped but the cave entrance was like a magnet pulling at him, enticing him inside.

'If this is what I'm here for, let's get it over with,' Killian mumbled and stepped over the threshold. He shuffled along the ground — every step echoed. After a while he stopped, still holding his wand in his outstretched hand. He decided to call out. 'Hello.' His voice travelled throughout and reverberated into the distance. 'Is there anybody there?' he continued, but the same thing happened again. 'I need to get out of here,' he said in a lower tone. 'I've got a case to solve and a beautiful woman waiting for me back home. I can't stay here. I don't need this.' He was talking to himself. He felt claustrophobic; not through fear of enclosed places, but fear of enclosed worlds — this one! He ran his tongue on the inside of his cheek, trying to think of some amazing plan, but nothing came. He thought to turn around and go back to the window outside the cave. What was he doing here? Who was calling him?

'What an idiot! What have you done this time Killian Spooks?' Why did you walk through that stupid fucking mirror?' He stopped talking when he heard something that made him shudder to his very core. The sound wasn't of a human kind. It was the deep, throaty growl of something much bigger. But it wasn't only the sound that frightened him. It was because the roar was so powerful that it echoed throughout the vast cave, and vibrated the ground to such an extent that Killian almost fell over. 'Oh-my-freaking-God,' he whimpered.

He froze, eyes bulging. He still couldn't see anything, but he knew that it wouldn't be long before he had a front row seat. He was panicking and found it difficult to breathe. Killian could feel his heart pounding in his throat and felt as though he was about to throw up. Soon the ground vibrated heavily to the thud-thud-thud of something so big that whatever got in its way wouldn't last much longer than a second. And that would be him soon enough.

Killian spun around with urgency and frantically held out his wand. The lighted tip shook violently, his nerves, making wavy, luminous lines in the blackness.

'I have to get outside and find that window again.' He grimaced, his stomach twisting in knots. The sound of the beast was getting closer and the wizard's confidence was at its weakest. Killian feverishly searched for an escape route so he could find somewhere safe to work out a plan. He didn't want to go deeper inside — what if there were more of these things in the bowels of this place? He knew in his heart of hearts that he had to either stand and fight or manoeuvre his way around. If he could do that then maybe he could find the window again and escape back home. But the beast was almost on him.

## Chapter 5
## The Beast

Killian strained his ears in a bid to try and pinpoint in which direction the beast was approaching, but he couldn't see far beyond the glare of his wand.

What he could see now were the deepened outlines of jagged rocks and boulders. They weren't visible before — what a strange world this was. He'd forgotten, being away so long. The rocks were all around, too high and smooth to simply try and climb out. He wouldn't have time. He had to hide right away and found a large gathering of boulders. Killian quickly dug in behind them and waited. He retracted his wand so that the light wouldn't give his position away, but he kept it at hand, ready to attack.

The heavy stomping of something massive entered the back end of the cavern and subsequently stopped. Killian sat quietly and didn't move a muscle. Why had it stopped? Why had it stopped? He kept running scenarios in his head. Then a thought hit him like a sledgehammer. Oh, my God. Could it smell him? If so, it would soon find him and well, he didn't want to think about it.

The stillness was all too consuming. Killian cowered down in the darkness, thinking the end of his life was near. Light suddenly appeared in the distance and threw a shadow on the wall behind him. The light flickered and Killian realised it was from a live flame. And so the movement of the creature continued all over again. Killian braved a peek over the top of the rock. Yes, it was a real flame all right. He also saw the beast for the first time and it wasn't alone… it had a rider.

The creature was huge. It appeared lizard-like with dark brown scales and mounted on each shoulder was a flaming stick. The light cast from the torches illuminated the monster's body but left its owner in silhouette. Killian looked on with wide eyes. How on Earth was it possible for the rider to tame a lizard? But then he remembered that he wasn't on Earth and anything was possible in this world. This doubled his challenge.

The eyes of the creature were big and round, about the size of a car wheel. From what he could make out they darted in quick, sharp, precise movements and covered a complete circle. Its head was wide with a long, narrow snout and some fins protruded from its top. It had breathtakingly, powerful shoulders, a huge barrel of a belly and

49

short, massive legs. Killian couldn't see whether it had a tail or not because the light didn't shine that far. The figure riding the beast sat upright and alert, pensive. Waiting for something. The smell from the creature soon hit Killian and it stank to high heaven.

Killian studied the movement of the rider on the saddle. It was weird, but Killian had a strange feeling that he knew him somehow. He gazed and shook his head.

'Just the worst thing when you recognise someone but can't remember,' Killian whispered. And then his fears were confirmed as the rider spoke...

'Hey, S-p-o-o-k-y. Where are you?' The rider called out in a sickly tone.

And Killian realised straight away who it was and what he was dealing with. He quickly dipped into his pocket and pulled out his mobile phone (not your ordinary cell phone — this one picked up supernatural signals from beyond). He urgently sent a message and put the phone back in his pocket, hoping the receiver would get it sooner rather than later. Killian swallowed down what spittle was left in his throat.

'Charlie Greech,' he whispered, 'so that's who was following and haunting me last night. That's who was taunting me at the station and in the park. I should have known. I thought something felt familiar about all this. Why didn't he confront me in my world? Perhaps he couldn't,' Killian reasoned. He was probably stronger in own environment, he assumed.

Charlie Greech was a scavenger and an enemy of Killian's from the dark world. They'd clashed on many occasions in the past. Killian eventually found a way to escape the world of the dead and broke out. He made a life for himself in the mortal world and never thought much of his old life. It had been so many years and the wizard hoped he'd never have to return. He certainly never thought he'd have to come across Charlie Greech ever again.

Killian suddenly realised why Charlie thought the wizard owed him something. It was because he had taken something from the scavenger, something that didn't belong to him. (That was what scavengers did in the dark world.) Now Killian assumed that Charlie wanted revenge for that. It all made sense now.

'So, he defeats me and keeps me here locked away in this God-forsaken world for the rest of eternity.' Killian winced at the thought. 'Well, that's not going to happen.'

Killian had another problem. Charlie Greech, he presumed, was probably in charge of this world now and that wasn't good news for the wizard or anybody else. Killian remembered that the dark world used to be run by Spade, an evil gravedigger who never crossed over. Killian had sent him on, to the other side. That was a place even worse than the world he was in right now. So Charlie Greech must have taken over Spade's throne. Killian could reason with Spade, but not with Greech. He realised he was in big trouble and needed help. He had to keep hidden for as long as he could manage. After all, Charlie Greech didn't know for sure if he was there.

'Come on, Spooky, show yourself,' Greech insisted, his voice irritating, like a saw cutting through tin. 'You know I'll find you eventually. Or I'll get Cruncher to trash this place until we do. You're not going anywhere this time. I have you.' As he spoke, he let out a huge, false belly laugh. Killian just closed his eyes in disbelief. Greech hadn't changed one bit. He was still a complete dick, but a very, powerful one.

'Cruncher, really?' Killian shook his head. What a stupid name for such a colossal brute. He had to chuckle to himself, even though he was in such grave danger. Charlie Greech didn't have any imagination. Killian pondered on that then it was back to reality and time to put a plan together. 'Think-think-think?' Killian probed his mind for some way out of this dire situation. Greech was dangerous but he was also quite stupid. And Killian had to come up with something a bit different. Suddenly his green eyes lit up like a light bulb and he mumbled a simple spell under his breath. There was a moment of silence, except for the slurping sound of the lizard's tongue as it slapped about on some rocks.

'Charlie Greech.' The voice came from everywhere in a low, hollow boom. The cave came alive. Charlie immediately shot upright in his saddle, trying to detect where the sound originated. The lizard creature flinched at the sudden, sharp sound and that almost dislodged the scavenger from his saddle. He gripped on tighter and tried to steady the beast.

'E-a-s-y, Cruncher, you fucking wimp,' Greech scolded and pulled on the reins. 'Big, useless lizard,' he mumbled under his breath. 'Where is that poor excuse for a wizard to then, hey?'

'You know not to call me Spooky, Greech, that only gets me annoyed — and you don't want to annoy me, remember?' Killian explained while projecting his voice. A wry smile curled across Charlie's face.

'Well, well, we meet again, Spooky. Where are you, my friend? I've missed you so much,' he said, the sarcasm dripping from every word. 'Come on, show yourself and we can hang out. Have a latte and some muffins,' Greech teased.

Killian narrowed his eyes. This guy was just as deluded as he'd always been. 'I've missed you too Greech… not!' Killian joked. 'So why don't you get down off that lovely, cuddly pet of yours and we could meet me face-to-face?' he said smoothly. 'We can discuss things in a normal and sensible way. And then I can kick your fucking arse.' But the wizard knew that wasn't going to happen.

Charlie let out another, full belly laugh and replied, 'No, no. I'm quite happy up here thank you,' he said politely and there was real fear in his tone. 'Why don't you get the fuck out here now and let me pummel you into the ground.' His high tone had changed to a growl and Killian could tell he was getting rattled, and that's what he intended. He'd had him wound up in the past and that shifted the advantage in Killian's favour.

Killian pondered his next move. He couldn't stall him forever. Charlie would soon click at what Killian was up to. Even Charlie Greech wasn't that stupid. The time had almost come to face him. All his wizard sense told him to stay put, but he didn't have a choice. All he needed to do was to carry the conversation a little bit longer… he hoped.

'Okay. You win, Greechy boy. I'll show myself,' Killian said. 'Oh, by the way, what is that lovely little animal you're riding? Did you get it from Ghouls 'R' Us?'

'Oh *Cruncher*,' Charlie explained, 'he's something I found wandering across the outlands. They call them swamp dogs, on account they stay close to swamps and kill everything they can find by roasting them alive. This one was injured and I fixed it, so it took a liking to me. I'm that kind of likeable guy,' he said, almost believing it himself.

'Wow. Are you listening to yourself? A likeable guy? You're a delusional, ugly, stinking scavenger. And that will never change,' Killian mused and then stopped. The fire breathing swamp dog gave him an idea. 'So, Cruncher, there can belch flames?'

'Oh yes, he can and will shortly, if you don't show yourself. Now get fucking out here so that I can barbecue you!' Greech screamed, his patience diminished. Killian walked out from the darkness into the light and stood, wand raised.

Charlie Greech was stunned for a moment. He didn't expect Killian to just step out into the open like that. The scavenger sat up with a start and grabbed one of the torches. It lit up his pale, gaunt face and shimmered against his spidery hair. Was it that simple? 'Crusher, *fire! Kill!*' The creature opened its mouth as wide as it could. It resembled a huge vice, with powerful jaws but no teeth. There was a rumble from deep within its belly, which travelled up into its throat and exploded in a firestorm of flames. And with the fire came a sickeningly, loud shriek — it was ear piercing. The wizard immediately put his hands up in surrender, but he stood no chance. The trail of heat was directed in an arc from side-to-side. The wild flames exploded a clump of trees, which were hidden in the shadow, but were now brightly, burning. The wizard had nowhere to run as his whole body was engulfed in a blaze of fierce flames and smoke. He was instantly charcoaled into a blackened spot, just a smudge on the ground. Greech looked on with wide, excited eyes.

'Well, that was easy,' Greech said, feeling a little cheated. He was expecting screaming and a roasted body running around like a headless chicken.

He immediately gave out the order for the swamp dog to stop. It did as asked, and the fire from within its mouth ceased, the last of the smoke evaporating from its throat and nostrils. The cave was now lit up in flowering flames from the stricken trees. 'Yes-yes-yes,' Charlie screeched triumphantly, laughing like someone possessed. He sat excitedly on the nape of the beast's neck, clapping wildly, his normally gaunt features filled with pride and happiness. 'I don't believe it. I've finally killed Killian Spooks — I've finally killed Killian Spooks,' he repeated in his usual squeaky voice. He began to repeat the same thing again and again. 'Killian Spooks is dead. Killian Spooks is dead. Killian Spooks is—' but he was cut short when the impact hit him so hard, that it knocked him clean out of his saddle. He went tumbling to the ground.

## Chapter 6
## Survival

Killian and Greech rolled down the swamp dog's back and tumbled off, freefalling through the air. They both landed awkwardly on the ground. Disorientated, they got to their feet and prepared to fight. It would be a battle in light and shadow, with the trees still burning with bright flames.

'I thought I'd killed you, wizard,' Charlie Greech groaned, shaking his head with distaste.

Killian didn't have his wand and must have lost it in the fall. He saw it in the dirt by his feet and immediately reached for it, but only managing to get his fingertips to it. Greech was wise to that and lunged at him, hitting him square in the chest with his shoulder. If they were playing rugby, it would have been a spectacular tackle. The crunching attack knocked the magical stick out of Killian's grasp. The two scrambled around on the ground and Charlie Greech saw his chance. The scavenger climbed on top of the wizard, gripped him around the throat and began to throttle him. But Killian slammed two rabbit punches to his midsection, which caught him unaware. The pain on his face was instantaneous. Greech crumpled and rolled off onto his back, which gave Killian a chance to get to his feet and search for his wand. He was about to call for it when he felt an arm wrap around his neck, cutting off his vocal cords.

They struggled for a few moments until Killian did a reverse head butt. He caught Charlie right on the bridge of his nose, breaking it with a bone-crunching crack, the blood gushing from his nostrils. He yelled out in pain as Killian whipped around and sent a powerful jab to his belly. The scavenger screamed and was thrown across the cave floor, landing in the dirt, sending dust flying up in a cloud.

Killian whispered under his breath and his wand soon appeared in his hand. He immediately pointed it at Charlie Greech, the tip crackling with energy.

'Don't move, Greech,' Killian said, his eyes wide and serious, 'or I'll cut you in half.'

'So, we've come to an impasse,' Charlie said. The light from the wizard's wand exposed the blood spilling down his mouth and chin.

'What do you mean?' Killian pressed. 'I don't understand.'

'Well, you want to kill me, right?' Charlie explained.

'Yes, obviously,' Killian nodded.

'I think you'll find old Cruncher there is waiting to charcoal your arse all over again,' Greech sniggered.

Killian looked up, still pointing his wand. Charlie was right — Cruncher was standing perfectly still, with eyes trained on him. Killian looked back at his enemy. 'So, I blow you away and you kill me too? Is that where this is leading?' Killian asked.

'Mmmmm, not sure yet,' Charlie Greech retorted.

'Okay. While we're on the subject, why didn't you try and kill me in my world?' Killian stalled. 'You had plenty of chances, so why didn't you?' he repeated.

'Because out there I didn't have the power I have in here,' he said. 'So the only way to get you back for all the stuff you've done to me in the past, was to bring you back here. So we could be on level terms. That's why I followed you and created that window.'

'How did you create that portal?' Killian was curious. 'It's all a bit above your level of intelligence, isn't it? I'm impressed.'

'Shut the fuck up, Spooks,' Greech exploded. 'I'm not as stupid as you think I am,' he countered and had to think about what he'd just said. Killian gave him a condescending grin and Greech sneered back in distaste. 'All right, it was always there,' he admitted. 'I found it and just popped through to where you were, and it opened. It's unstable and moves around on its own. Where it is now is anyone's guess and for how long it stays there is just as unpredictable. I have no control over it, but it doesn't matter because you're here and the window is not. So, you're fucked,' he said with satisfaction. 'You'll be dead before it appears again and won't be able to go back.'

This shook Killian to the core. This was one thing Charlie Greech was right about. If Greech killed him, even though he was a wizard, he couldn't return to his world ever again! Killian had to box clever. The only real tool he held against the scavenger was wisdom.

'How do you know that this is me?' Killian said with a smile. 'I mean, you've just killed me once and it was only an image, so how do you know it's me now?'

Greech mulled it over and came back with, 'If you're not you, then I'll kill whatever is standing there right now and search for more of you,' Greech reasoned. 'It doesn't matter in my world. I'll get you in the end. You're not going back, Spooks, I'll make sure of it.' He sounded too confident and Killian didn't like that. This was his

61

world and Killian hadn't been back in many years. Greech knew this world in and out, and Killian did not. The thought of never going back home scared the hell out of him.

'Wow, what happened to you? You sound intelligent for once,' Killian mocked. This made Charlie Greech wince. 'So, after I got rid of Spade, you took over, did you?' Killian said, still stalling for time.

'I'm in charge and I have been for years, Spooky. This is my world and you are mine.' And there it was again. Killian hated him calling him Spooky, but he couldn't stop him and that was the least of his problems right now.

'I didn't think you were bright enough to run a whole world on your own, Greech. Your subjects must be really stupid to follow you,' Killian continued. He was talking and trying to work out a way back — it was exhausting.

'I fucking hate you, Spooks. Always have, always will, so I think it's time to end this little party, once and for all. Prepare to die, my friend.'

Killian stood firm but was bricking it. He couldn't bluff his way out any longer. If anything was going to happen — it had to happen now. This was it.

'Let's get this over with,' Killian said calmly. Charlie Greech stood up but quickly hid behind a rock. Killian didn't have him for a target any longer and with that, Greech gave the order again.

'Cruncher,' he said smugly, '*fire! Kill!*' He spoke the words with relish. The swamp dog obeyed immediately and opened its mouth, and the familiar rumble of energy began to build in its stomach. Killian winced when he felt a sharp pain in his hand and instantly dropped the wand. The rock Charlie had thrown had hit its target and left the wizard helpless. Killian looked at the giant lizard with its wide jaws — there was nowhere to go. This was it!

Suddenly, a loud flapping sound filled the air and that caught the attention of the beast. It was poised to belch fire at the wizard, but for a second or so held back. Even with that distraction, Killian had nothing to shield himself from the furnace. His existence was about to come to an end and Charlie Greech laughed out loud engrossed at how terrified the wizard appeared.

'Die, Spooky, die!' he cackled like an old witch. 'You fucking menace.' But when he saw that his pet was preoccupied, he let rip. 'Fire, kill, you stupid lizard,' he screamed.

But, from out of nowhere, a huge set of razor-sharp jaws appeared, only exposed by the flowering fires in the cave. This was followed by high-pitched squeals that echoed throughout the vast, cavern. The lizard was distracted and the flames that were bubbling in its throat didn't leave its mouth. The bird creature soon revealed itself fully. It was colossal, with a long, cigar-shaped head and slick, black, leathered skin. Its milky eyes glistened in the reflection of the flames. The wingspan easily covered the length of the lizard's whole body. And as quickly as it appeared, it lunged at the swamp beast and gripped its neck with its large, powerful beak. The lizard was taken completely by surprise.

The pterodactyl tore into its neck, the bird's razor-sharp incisors cutting through the soft tissue of its throat. Once the ancient had established its authority, it clambered onto the lizard's back and sunk its talon's deep into the monster's mid-riff. It ripped through the outer protective scales, to the tender skin inside; blood gushed from the open wounds. The swamp dog let out a blood-curdling shriek. It twisted its neck and tried to dislodge the ancient creature from attacking the nape of its neck, the look in its eyes one of pure horror. It thrashed its mighty, whipping tail, cutting through rock and tree. It wriggled and squirmed and attempted to flip over, but the huge bird dug in deeper. The bird had locked on and was tearing deeper and deeper into its thick, wide neck. Soon jagged holes appeared, filled with sinewy, muscle and free-flowing black blood. The razor-edged teeth ripped and slashed easily and the bird screeched in victory. The cumbersome giant was too clumsy to defend itself and no matter what it did, it didn't matter. It was pitiful to watch as the wild fight continued. The lizard creature let out another feeble screech and the piercing sound made Killian clamp his hands over his ears. The dinosaur bird was relentless and continued ripping, tearing and gouging, deeper and deeper inside the swamp dog's throat.

The beast was slowing down, its fight almost at an end, the blood spilling to the ground, pooling around it like a small lake. It only took a matter of minutes before the attacking bird cut right through the neck and crushed it inside its throat with a mighty snap. The huge, vice-like jaws clamped shut until the top and bottom teeth met. The swamp dog's body went limp and no more sound left its mouth.

Killian ran out of the way as it slowly crumpled to the ground and rolled onto its side. The whole cave shook as clouds of dust billowed out from underneath its almost headless body, which was only held on by sinew. The fire-breathing monster was no more and the bird stopped attacking when it knew the swamp dog was dead. Everything quietened down from the frenzy of pitiful shrieks. Now only the gentle crackle of the burning trees and the trickle of loose debris remained.

Greech looked on in devastation as the head broke away from its torso and tumbled to the ground next to its remains, the eyes still open but devoid of life, and its tongue flopped loosely from the corner of its mouth. Killian climbed out from behind a boulder and stood by the side of the carcass, he stooped down and retrieved his wand from the dirt. The giant dinosaur bird had already morphed back into the monk that was Zoot. He stood in his blackened robe, saturated in the glistening, black blood of the beast. He looked at Killian and nodded, but the warlock could see how much it had taken out of his friend. He was gaunt — his eyes heavy — his body physically trembling.

'Rest, my friend,' Killian said and turned to Charlie Greech, but he'd already disappeared. Killian was mortified. He wasn't going to lose him again.

'Where the fuck, has he gone?' Killian urgently looked around, wand still in hand, but there were too many dark places in which he could hide and escape.

'Greech! Greech! Where are you, you bastard?' the sorcerer ranted.

'What now, Killian? Forget him, he's gone. How on earth are we going to get back?' Zoot called out weakly.

'The only problem is, we're not on Earth. We have to find the window again. Where did you get in?' Killian asked.

'It's not far from here. Or at least it felt like it. This place can play tricks on you,' Zoot admitted. 'I never thought I'd have to come back to this horrible place.'

'I know, and I thank you for coming to my aid, Zoot,' Killian said humbly. 'I honestly wouldn't have called you if I thought I could handle it myself.'

'I got your call, Killian, and I promised I'd never let you down,' Zoot said sincerely. 'The signal got me to the window and the rest is, well, you know?'

'I thought I was a goner for sure this time. But saying that, we haven't got out of here yet. And believe me, I want to get home as much as you do,' he admitted.

'Let's get out of here and find that window then,' Zoot pressed.

'I'm with you on that one, my friend,' Killian agreed. 'I'm hoping that it's still there.'

'This way,' Zoot said and pointed to the way he came in.

'No time like the present,' Killian said and they walked away, leaving the beast to its new burial ground. Zoot was a bit frail and Killian supported his friend as they stumbled through the darkness with the wand leading the way. Time was running out and Killian knew that window wouldn't last forever. If it disappeared then the two of them were stuck in the dark world for eternity.

# Chapter 7
## Where's the Window?

Zoot and Killian moved through the darkness without interruption. The scary people in the shadows recognised the wizard from his time there in the past and stayed away. Killian retraced his steps to the place of entry. When they'd got there, he realised that it wasn't that far from the cave.

'This is it — this is the place,' Killian said in bewilderment.

'Yep, this is where I crossed over too,' Zoot agreed. The two of them stood in an open space, but the mirror wasn't anywhere to be seen. There was no evidence — not a ripple or distortion. 'Where's the window, Killian?' Zoot asked with concern. 'I don't see it anywhere. Are we stuck here for good?'

Killian, for once, didn't have a Plan B. 'I don't know, but it has to be somewhere around here.' He was grasping at straws. He'd lost Charlie Greech and that was bad enough. 'I'm sure Greech won't be far behind us.' Killian shivered at the thought.

'I've heard you speak of that mongrel when we've had our little talks over tea,' Zoot said. 'I never expected to meet him though.'

'Yeah, well he's more powerful than ever now,' Killian sighed. 'We have to get out of here right now before he gathers his scavenger buddies to block our way. There are only two of us and he has the whole world to choose from.'

'That doesn't sound good,' Zoot agreed.

'It's not. Let's go back,' Killian said.

'Are you seriously suggesting that we go back to that awful cave?' Zoot said, screwing up his blood-soaked face. Killian's eyes widened and a sly grin curled his lip. Of course, he thought.

'I have an idea where we can find the window,' Killian said with confidence.

'Well, that sounds more positive. But the cave, really?' Zoot complained.

'Shut up and let me concentrate,' Killian ordered. He grabbed his phone and brought up his GPS. Zoot looked at him in disbelief.

'Are you serious? That's your plan? Using a satellite navigation to guide us out of here?' Zoot was mystified. 'Why don't you call for roadside assistance while you're at it?' he mocked. 'I'm sure lots of people know where the Land of the Dead is.'

Killian looked at him through the flames of the burning trees. 'Are you finished?' he responded. 'Have you got a better idea?' he snarled, but Zoot didn't utter a word. 'Thought not. Come on, it's this way,' he insisted and grinned. Zoot shrugged his shoulders but followed anyway. He moved after Killian through the darkness. The wizard was holding his wand in one hand to light the way and his phone in the other. They manoeuvred around the fallen lizard and moved further into the depths of the cave.

Zoot peeked over the wizard's shoulder at the screen. He could see a flashing, yellow dot. He could not believe what he was witnessing and had to ask. 'What is that?' he quizzed. 'Is the window coming up on a digital screen?'

Killian turned and stared at the monk, with a look of disbelief. 'Are you serious right now? You think that this dot is the window?'

Zoot just shrugged his shoulders. 'What is it then? Come on Killian, give me a clue?'

'That my friend is my homing stone,' Killian said with pride and Zoot suddenly understood what all the activity was about. He burst out laughing.

'You brilliant, brilliant wizard,' he gushed with joy. 'So you have a homing stone. Hopefully, then, it won't only locate where the window is —

71

it should also keep it stable on the other side,' Zoot responded. 'Clever.'

'Wow, now you're getting it,' Killian said with a condescending smile and then his face changed. 'Let's just hope it works. The window has obviously moved on our end.'

'Okay. Is it far?' Zoot chipped in.

'Not according to this, but we don't know what lies between us and it. Or, we do know, but don't want to know, if you know what I mean?' Killian blurted.

'Uh, well, er. Okay,' Zoot agreed, but he didn't understand what his friend was telling him.

'You can guarantee that Charlie Greech is out there waiting.' Killian heaved a depressed sigh. He just wanted to get back home, but he knew that it wasn't going to be that simple — things were never that simple.

They travelled through tunnels where water dripped and strange things shuffled about all around them. The wand gave light but the two of them were relieved when they saw natural light spilling in from outside. It wasn't bright like daylight. There was never daylight in the land of nothing, only twilight. Killian peered at the screen and looked up. They were surrounded by mountains and murky-looking grey skies above. Killian breathed steadily and didn't speak. It felt good to be outside again, but what was waiting for them?

'What is it?' Zoot asked him urgently. 'Are you okay, Killian?'

'It's this place. Never thought I'd have to come back here. Everything is too familiar. I hated it when I was here last. And I loathe it even more now.'

'Where do we need to go? It can't be far,' Zoot said, trying to lend moral support and get his friend's spirits up.

'It's just beyond that clearing,' Killian said, sounding a little more upbeat. They scurried along in the semi-darkness, walking parallel to each other on a rocky ledge. Killian was checking the screen on his phone when Zoot stopped and grabbed Killian's arm.

'Oh boy,' Zoot sighed and Killian looked into his face. He was staring at something and he slowly followed his line of sight.

'Shit.' Killian grimaced, and grabbed Zoot and hit the ground. He quickly turned off his phone and extinguished his wand.

'Exactly,' Zoot agreed.

Killian looked at the open ground below. It was a vast area, which seemed to go on for miles. And every centimetre was obscured with hordes of scavengers — you couldn't put a toothpick

73

between them. If it hadn't been for the intermittently placed flaming torches, Killian and Zoot would have walked right into them. And another strange thing was, the fact that even though there were thousands of the zombie-like creatures there — not a sound could be heard.

'Why didn't he keep it dark down there? We'd have been captured right away and we'd have walked right into them,' Zoot explained.

'Because he wants to make sure he can see us, so that we can't slip past him, I suppose,' Killian assumed.

'Why has he assembled there? The mirror must be nearby,' Zoot said.

'Exactly, Zoot. Look over there.' Killian's eyes were wide and filled with hope.

'What? Oh yeah.' Zoot was smiling. Just beyond the masses was a shimmering disk that hung in the air like a beautiful silvery painting. It was their escape route. Its brilliance cut a large, white, circular frame through the gloom of the dark world. It was so near, yet so depressingly far too.

'Jesus… can't we catch a fucking break?' Killian growled. 'Greech must have known where it was all this time.'

'Killian,' Zoot scolded, 'you're in the presence of a monk, don't forget.'

'Oh, sorry for the swearing, Zoot, but it does paint a rather dismal picture. Oh, by the way I'm going to curse again,' he grunted. 'Let's face it. Things look pretty fucking dire if you ask me,' Killian conceded.

'Nobody is really asking you at this point, are they?' Zoot peered back through half-opened eyes.

'Well—'

But Zoot put up a hand to stop him before he spoke. Killian was about to throw one of the biggest tantrums when Zoot quickly spoke. 'I've got a plan... I think it'll work,' Zoot announced. He was rolling his bald head from side to side as if he was still putting it together. 'It does involve leaving the ground for both of us,' Zoot continued.

'I hate flying — you know that.' Killian spoke up instantly.

'I know,' Zoot responded. 'I don't like motor scooters either, but hey-ho.'

'I repeat — I hate flying,' Killian snapped.

'We don't have a choice, do we?' Zoot reminded him. 'Do you want to get out of this place?' Killian did his best snarly face and begrudgingly nodded. 'Well. It's the only way I can think of. If it works,' Zoot said.

'I still hate flying,' Killian repeated and knew this wasn't going to change anything.

'Have you another suggestion?' Zoot probed. 'I'm all ears.' There was silence from the wizard. 'I thought as much. Flying it is then?'

He was smiling a little too much for Killian's liking. He was getting him back for all the bike rides Killian had taken him on.

'Yeah... okay,' Killian agreed with a weighty sigh. 'What do you have in mind?

'Well...' Zoot told the wizard his plan and there was a nod here and there.

'Mmmm,' Killian added when the information was relayed to him.

'What do you think?' Zoot waited.

'Okay. It may work,' Killian reluctantly agreed.

'It's all we have,' Zoot said, with a hint of desperation to his tone. 'Let's find somewhere a bit more hidden.'

'Okay. Let's do it. I've got nothing,' Killian admitted. They walked back until they were out of sight from the enemy. Killian stood back as Zoot concentrated. Soon he was evolving, morphing into something big. Killian looked on in awe as he always did when his friend contorted into some amazing form. It only took a matter of seconds before Zoot was no more, and a large dragon stood before him. The beautiful beast rose. It had a huge, blue scaly body, with wings folded neatly at his side. Zoot's head was narrow at the snout with two large, black eyes. He had long, sharp talons, which protruded from five-fingered claws. He was magnificent.

'Wow,' Killian breathed. The dragon winked at him.

'Wow indeed,' Zoot said and that was always completely weird when a dragon talked back to you. 'Climb on, Killian.' Zoot dropped his head to the ground, allowing the wizard to climb on board.

Killian reluctantly clambered up the dragon's neck, still mumbling that he hated heights and flying. 'They're not going to just let us pass. You know that, right?' Killian said as he settled in.

'Nothing is ever easy in any world, Killian,' Zoot replied and the giant creature unfurled its wings and soon lifted off the ground. Killian could feel his knuckles whiten as he gripped onto Zoot's scales. He closed his eyes as tightly as he could and sat rigidly. 'It's okay Killian — we're already flying,' Zoot informed him. Killian opened his eyes and looked down and gripped on even tighter if that were possible.

'Did I mention I hate flying?' he repeated.

'Only about a million times. Now shut up and hold on,' Zoot instructed.

'Expect anything. I know you've been here before, Zoot, but as you know, anything can happen in this foul place,' Killian said seriously. 'They'll attack from any angle.'

'Got it,' Zoot agreed. He swooped from the mountain ridge and they descended the valley towards the shimmering exit. The dragon swept in at great speed, making Killian's cheeks ripple with the G-force. The sheer rush of air was deafening and soon the wizard was starting to enjoy the experience. As they levelled off, the full scale of Charlie Greech's army greeted them. Killian could feel a deep vibration from within the dragon's belly. It travelled up into its throat and eventually belched a line of yellow fire, which ripped a corridor through the hoard of scavengers.

The heat from the flames washed over his face like a giant hair-dryer. He pressed himself as tight as he could to Zoot's neck, to avoid being singed and charcoaled. The scavengers were scorched away in an explosion of heat and flame, their bodies incinerated into brown dust. Zoot surged forward, parallel to the ground, and spewed another stream of the devastating fire. More of the zombie army were burned to ashes. The rest could see what was coming but had nowhere to run in time as the dragon continued its destruction.

'This is too easy.' Killian spoke softly, the rush of wind taking his words.

Zoot was about to unleash another spray of flames. 'We're almost there, Killian,' he said excitedly. Suddenly, there were noises from above and as Killian looked up his eyes almost bulged from their sockets.

'Zoot, look out,' he screamed. Large rocks came raining down on top of them like hail. Suddenly, one large rock struck the dragon's shoulder. Zoot let out a screech of pain. Another caught his tail but luckily ricocheted off harmlessly. 'Left-left,' Killian bellowed, 'quickly.' Zoot realised what he meant and just about managed to bank left to avoid another collision with a sharp, football-sized boulder.

'We have to get out of here or we'll get pummelled,' Killian shrieked.

'We're almost there, Killian,' Zoot called back. 'Almost there.'

Killian urgently dipped into his pocket and retrieved his wand. He quickly aimed and fired a series of blasts. The attacking scavengers instantly exploded, peppering the sky with brown dirt.

'How are they flying?' Zoot yelled. 'I can't see them from this angle.'

'There are no rules to this world, Zoot. They can fly too,' Killian shouted back. 'We have to get to that window before Charlie comes up with something that we won't be able to handle,' he added gravely. He used his wand to set off another barrage of blasts and the scavengers were pushed back, but only temporarily.

'We're getting close,' Zoot announced, 'only a few more seconds and we'll be free,' he said with glee.

'I'll hold these off for as long as I can and you concentrate on targeting that window. If we miss it, I don't think we'll ever leave this place again,' Killian screamed in his ear.

Zoot let loose with another trail of fire and they both heard the screams from Charlie, shouting from below. He was ranting on a ledge above the battle, like some wild dictator. 'Kill the fuckers! Don't let them fucking escape,' he raged. 'Kill-kill-kill!' He was waving his arms like a windmill and shouting.

Killian could suddenly feel there was something wrong. The dragon's wings had ceased flapping and it was veering off course. Then Killian could see the problem - Zoot was bleeding from a gash on top of his head; he was unconscious.

'Shit,' Killian gasped. They were dipping down towards the swarm of scavengers on the ground. They were going to crash.

# Chapter 8
## Locked Away

The great dragon came down and crash-landed with a huge impact. It carved a trench through the dirt as it went ploughing across the ground. Scavengers fled but some were unlucky and were crushed under the dragon's belly. It finally came to a stop in a cloud of dust and debris. Killian could see it all unfolding in front of him and braced for impact. As soon as the dragon began to roll over — he took his chance and jumped off, landing awkwardly, which knocked the wind out of his lungs.

He tried to catch his breath, but the dust hit the back of his throat and he coughed violently, his face reddened. He recovered as quickly as he could and clambered to his feet, still clutching his wand. He was disorientated as he stood inside the dust cloud. When the powder finally settled, Killian realised that he was completely surrounded.

'Shit,' he grimaced. He raised his wand in defence, but thought better of it when he saw a group of scavengers pooling around Zoot, with weapons ready to pummel him. Zoot had morphed back and was unconscious, his robe lying by his side. Killian realised that if he did anything now, they would kill his friend instantly — he couldn't take that risk.

'Well, well-well,' came the familiar voice of Charlie Greech and the scavengers parted a corridor for their master to walk through. 'What do we have here?' he said smugly. 'The great Killian Spooks, slayer of demons… captured!' Killian said nothing. A scavenger stepped forward from the others and ripped the wand from the wizard's hand. Now he was defenceless. Greech nodded for two of his men to grab Killian's arms. He leaned in; his body stank of decay, his breath rank. Killian winced and tried to pull away, but he was held fast. 'Hello, prick,' he said and lashed out with his right fist. He caught the wizard on the side of his face with a heavy blow. Killian's whole head snapped to one side, blood instantly seeping from a fresh cut below his left eye.

Killian scowled. 'You'll fucking pay for that, Greech,' he said as he creased up his face.

Charlie Greech was in full laughter mode when he let rip with another punch — right at his jaw this time. The force almost gave Killian whiplash as his head snapped back. The sorcerer screamed in pain, to which Greech kept on giggling.

'You sick fuck,' Killian spat, the blood freely running down his chin.

He pushed his face right next to Killian's and said in a whisper, 'You're not getting away this time, Spooky. Time to die, I think. I'm going to enjoy this.' The nerves in Killian's stomach tightened at the thought of what was going to happen next.

The evil master beckoned to one of his men to hand him a spear. He gripped it and weighed the weapon in both hands, and smiled. He gazed lovingly at the long, sharp spike. 'This should do nicely,' he said with a pleasant grin, still happy at getting his prize wizard.

What a way to go, Killian thought, but stood firm and waited for the inevitable. He waited as Charlie pointed the spear at his gut to impale him. A scavenger appeared at his side and whispered something in his ear. Charlie's attitude changed from delight to a dark grimace. Something was wrong and it may have just saved Killian's life. Charlie Greech looked deeply into Killian's eyes and handed the spear back to one of his minion's. 'Put them in the fucking cells,' he snapped. 'I'll finish this conversation later.' His henchmen said nothing as they grabbed the wizard and led him away. They also took the monk and dragged him along the ground. Killian tugged and pulled but the filthy creatures held on tight. He watched as Charlie went in another direction, his troops parting for him to walk through. Where's he going in such a hurry? Killian pondered. It buys us time, he thought again, but for how long?

Killian was led to somewhere he'd never been before. It looked to be a small, shabby western town. Not unlike a place from the eighteen hundreds, where cowboys and cattle wranglers would stay for a night and get a drink. Everything looked grim in this world, especially in this semi-darkness. Killian looked to his left and saw the scavengers dragging Zoot through along the ground, his body covered in white dust.

'Lift him up, you fucking morons,' Killian burst out with a low, growl and his eyes glowed green. The zombie-like soldiers appeared scared of the wizard and did as they were asked, lifting the monk up off his feet. Killian's eyes returned to normal in a flash.

The Scavengers led the prisoners to a medium-sized building, which oddly enough resembled a western-style jail. It reminded Killian of old cowboy movies from the Wild West, where the sheriff would imprison outlaws. This was surreal.

Greech must have a fixation with the old West, Killian assumed.

Without any spoken word, a scavenger stepped up onto the porch and opened the wooden door to the building. There were three metal cages inside, each with thick bars securing them. At the back of one of the cells and high up on the wall was a small window. It was too small to climb through, and that too held solid, iron rods. Zoot was put in the middle cell, still unconscious. Killian was placed in the first cage. They put Zoot gently on the small bed in the cell. They didn't want to offend Killian who was watching over their every move. Both the cells were locked and one scavenger put the keys on a hook against the back wall.

Killian kept an eye on the other guard, who still held his wand. He noticed that that guy placed it inside a box on the desk. Killian smiled with satisfaction. The keys were just behind the desk on the wall and his wand was in a box on the desk. He reasoned that once Greech's goons were gone, then he could call the wand out of the box and they could escape — piece of cake. The instant the lid closed though, Killian couldn't *feel* the connection with his magic any longer and his smile faded. He sighed.

Fair play, Greech had thought of everything. The guards left the building and the wizard stood in the darkness. He immediately tried to conjure a spell to unlock the cage door, but his magic wouldn't come, just like his wand — he couldn't feel it any more. He was stuck and his mind wandered on to other things. Why didn't Charlie kill him there and then? he reasoned. What was going on? He looked around at the space he was in. It was a three-metre by two-metre box. There was a makeshift bench-bed to his left and... that was it. He'd never felt so depressed in his life. Could he actually make it out of this world? Or was he just kidding himself. Anyway, that wasn't his priority at the minute. He needed to wake up Zoot to make sure he was okay. Once he was awake, they could work on a plan together. Two heads were better than one.

'Zoot. Zoot, wake up man,' Killian hissed through the darkness. He couldn't get a response. He tried to reach him by putting his arms through the bars. He groaned as he strained, but it was no use — he was too far to the other side of the cell. '*Zoot!* Please wake up, mate,' Killian pleaded, but nothing.

Killian knew he'd received quite a bump to the head and realised that he might be out for hours. Hours they didn't have. Killian slumped to the floor and that's when his own pain kicked in. The left side of his head felt like a balloon. He gingerly touched it with his hand. His jaw wasn't so bad, but his eyes seemed quite thick to touch. He didn't have a mirror to check out the damage that Greech had caused. Killian was going to murder that fucking mongrel. 'Zoot, come on man, we have to get out of here,' he half whispered. He finally gave up and sat on the bed. This was going nowhere. That was when he heard a commotion from outside of his cell window. He jerked upright on the bed. There were screams of pain from the scavengers outside somewhere. He climbed up from the bed and pushed his feet on tiptoe to see what was happening. The window was only small but was wide enough to give Killian some kind of visibility.

He could see lots of panicked bodies moving in different directions as if scared. Killian had seen confusion like this before and realised that things were in disarray. Something was coming and Charlie's army were being roused. What could possibly throw Charlie Greech into panic mode? And then it hit him like a slap across the face with a wet kipper. The first person that Killian could think of was Spade.

But then he remembered that it couldn't be Spade. From what Killian remembered, from the last time he was here, Spade was dead. So who was attacking Greech now? There must be another enemy out there — one, who was as powerful as Charlie Greech. Otherwise, Greech wouldn't be this panicked. Killian wracked his brains to remember who else was capable of attacking the scavengers but came up empty. It didn't matter anyway He had to get out of this place, but with Zoot still out, what could he do?

'Zoot. Zoot,' Killian screamed with more intensity. 'Wake up-wake up! For fuck's sake, Zoot, *wake up!*' But it was no use. Killian was out of options and slumped on his bed again. He looked at the box on the desk that contained his wand. Damn, it was so close yet he was useless without it. He tried calling it with his mind, but it just wasn't working. Nothing he tried was working, until…

'Er, hello. Maybe I can help.'

Killian tensed, holding his breath for a few seconds, eyes wide. He rested his elbows on his bed and squinted through the grainy haze that filled the room. He couldn't see anything in this level of light.

'Hello,' uttered the soft voice again. 'Would you like me to rouse your friend?'

Killian didn't know what to say at first. And then he plucked up the courage to talk. 'Who are you? Where are you?' Killian spoke in a slow, unwavering manner.

'I'm in the last cell, next to your friend,' the man said.

'If you're a spy, then make sure you escape away from me because I'll hunt you down.'

And with that came one of the biggest belly-laughs that he'd ever heard before. Killian could see some movement, but nothing solid. This guy was really strange. Who was he and how could he help them?

'Oh, no, no, my friend. I may be a lot of things, but snitch isn't one of them, I promise. Now do you want my help, or not? Time is tight.'

'The answer to that is yes, definitely,' Killian responded. 'I just, need to know who you are before we go any further?' Killian probed cautiously.

'Look, let's sort out our escape first,' the stranger retorted.

# Chapter 9
## Flint

'Now is not the time for introductions. We've very little time,' the voice continued. 'Greech had me captured and thrown in here a few days ago. I think he wanted to come back and kill me personally, but was occupied by other things. Then there was talk of a *wizard* who was going to invade this world. I take it that was you? Greech hasn't had time to finish me off yet,' the guy said.

Killian sat in the dark, mystified. 'I've been the main news in this place for the last few days?' he asked, astonished at the statement. 'I've been away for so long that I thought I'd have been forgotten.'

'Yeah, so you *are* Killian Spooks? They think that you're some kind of Messiah. You've already saved my life once, so I'm returning the favour,' the stranger said happily. 'I'm sorry, but I don't know who you are,' the stranger continued.

'That's fine. I'm no one really,' Killian replied. 'How do I know you're not setting us up?' he pressed, keen to know what answer he was going to give.

'Really, you're asking me that? We're in a prison and I'm going to lead you to Greech and his pals? Is that what you think?' The stranger sounded angry.

Killian mulled it over and came up with the reasoning that this guy had nothing to gain. He was already locked up, so why would he be helping Charlie Greech? 'All right, I believe you, I apologise. I'm a wizard. Why can't I get my magic to work in here?' Killian complained. 'This has never happened before.'

'It's muted inside this cage,' the stranger said. 'Charlie Greech is getting wise in his old age.'

'You have powers too?' Killian questioned.

'Don't worry about me, wizard, we've other fish to fry,' he answered.

'What do you have in mind?' Killian asked, intrigued. 'We need to act fast.'

'Your friend there — he's a shape-shifter, isn't he?' the stranger said.

'Yes, he is. How do you know? You seem to know a lot of stuff, mister,' Killian said. He didn't like the idea that this guy knew a lot about him and Zoot, and he knew nothing about him. 'Again, who are you?'

'Look, I haven't time to fully explain. But there was word that a wizard tried to escape on a dragon. You're the wizard, so your friend there

91

has got to be a shape-shifter, am I right?' the stranger asked.

This all made sense and all Killian was doing was stalling for time. Time, which they didn't have. 'Okay,' Killian bit back, 'so what's the plan?' Killian was sitting upright and alert, straining to see through the darkness. He just couldn't see any detail, only a silhouette.

'We wake up your friend and see if we can get him to morph into something like, maybe a snake or something? If so, he can slither to the keys on the hook and bring them back here. Sound good?' the man said with purpose.

It was a good idea actually, but Killian didn't want this guy taking all the glory and having one over on him. And time was of the essence. Charlie Greech could be back at any moment and finish them all off. There were no other options. 'It sounds all right to me. Wait. Hold on, why would my friends' powers work inside here? Does the damper field work on Shapeshifters too?' He could be just as incapacitated as we are, don't you think?' Killian assumed.

'To be honest, I'm not sure. Your guess is as good as mine. If he can't, then we're all fucked,' the stranger said blatantly. 'We have to try something.'

'Wake him up then,' Killian said simply. 'He's our only hope to get out of here.'

'Hey, fella,' the man shouted. 'Hey, mister…'

'Zoot. His name is Zoot,' Killian said.

'Sorry. Hey, Zoot. Come on guy,' the man called out and stretched his arm through the bars and violently tugged at Zoot's robe. 'Wake up, man — we need you,' he rasped. Killian could only see the guy's outline. He could also hear the groans of his friend, Zoot, slowly regaining consciousness.

'Wake up, my friend.' He called urgently, until Zoot slowly opened his eyes. But that soon changed when suddenly he was dowsed with water. The monk came around, much quicker — spitting out water from his mouth. The stranger gave a heavy giggly and tossed the jug to one side.

'What-the…' Zoot spat, almost choking. 'What's going on? Oh, I feel sick.' Zoot heaved and threw up chunks in the corner of the cell.

'Yuk,' the man responded.

'Hey, Zoot. Are you okay? Welcome back, mate,' Killian called out from his cell.

'Arrrgh, my head,' Zoot complained rubbing the back of his skull. He gradually sat up on his bed. 'I don't feel good at all,' he groaned.

93

'We haven't got time for that shit, fella,' the stranger grunted from his cell. 'You need to act fast.'

'What? Who are you?' Zoot asked immediately, trying to make sense of everything. 'Killian. Who is this moron?'

'Moron, why, you little fucker,' the stranger ranted.

'Don't worry about him, Zoot. We've got more pressing stuff, like not dying for starters,' Killian expressed. 'We need you to help us get out of here.'

'Killian. Are you okay?' Zoot asked his friend. 'What happened to the mirror?'

'Oh, for fuck's sake. Can we please dispense with the meet and greet, and get on with this?' the man pressed.

'Yeah, I'm fine, Zoot. Don't take any notice of Mr Grumpy Chops over there. The mirror is the least of our problems at the moment.' Killian said. 'Do you think you can morph right away?'

'Yeah, I guess so. I'm still a bit wobbly but I should be fine,' Zoot agreed. 'What do you need?'

'There are keys on a hook, just beyond the desk,' the stranger informed him.

'Can you change into something that can quickly get through those bars, morph back and unlock our cells?' Killian asked him.

'I can do better than that,' he said and with that began to concentrate. He reached out with his arm, through the bars, and when he'd gone as far as he could, suddenly, his arm began to elongate farther out. It looked hideous as it stretched and got thinner, making it deform into a child-like limb. Killian could just about make it out in the grainy, haze and winced.

'That's it. You're doing it. Yes-yes-yes,' the stranger boomed excitedly.

'Yeah, go on, Zoot,' Killian encouraged. Zoot strained as he worked his arm into a long, thin tree-like limb. Sweat poured down his dirty face as he stretched.

'You're nearly there,' the stranger said with glee.

'Keep going, my friend,' Killian whispered under his breath. Zoot stopped when he felt the metal with his fingertips and steadily lifted the ring off the hook. Just as he did so, the wizard heard footsteps heading towards the jail.

'Shit, someone's coming. Hurry Zoot,' Killian rasped.

Zoot was working as fast as he could. He was retracting his extended arm and had almost got it back to normal. He was just about to put the key in the lock when the guards entered the jail and Zoot lost his grip.

At first, they didn't register what was happening. The prisoners were still locked away safely in their cells, but when one of them looked for the keys, he realised that they weren't on the hook. One looked at the other and they both immediately understood what had happened. They charged at Zoot's cage to take him away, but before they'd even had a chance to do anything… the two of them instantly burst into a large ball of flames and exploded. Zoot looked on totally shocked. Killian stumbled back in his cell so as not to get toasted.

'What the fuck just happened?' Killian called out dryly, still reeling in shock.

'I-I don't know…' Zoot garbled the words as they both looked in the direction of the stranger. He was already out of his cell. He'd sneakily grabbed the keys that Zoot had dropped on the floor.

'Hi, gentlemen,' he said as he unlocked each of their cages. 'I'm Flint and as you can see, Flint by name and fire by nature.' He said it as though he'd done so a million times. He was of medium height with grey eyes and a full head of hair. His thick, grey beard meshed seamlessly into the grey mop on top of his head and you couldn't see where it started or finished. He wore a big, brown overcoat and tan boots. If Killian didn't know any better, he would have said he looked exactly like... Santa Claus.

'I guess there's no need to explain why you have that name, is there? Your powers work outside the cage, I see. There must be a damper field in these cells, like you said,' Killian remembered.

'Yeah, they must neutralise magic somehow, clever,' Flint added.

'Nice to meet you, Flint,' Zoot said, sticking out his hand, still a bit in awe.

'You too, my monk friend.' Flint grabbed Zoot's hand and gave a vigorously hard shake. 'You're the first monk I've ever met, son,' Flint admitted and turned to Killian.

'Yeah, you're the first Flint I've ever met,' Killian added, but reluctantly gripped his hand. Flint gave out a chuckle.

'Don't worry, Killian Spooks, I promise that I won't turn you into a fireball,' Flint said, still giggling.

'You seem to know a lot of things about me, Flint,' Killian said, peering straight into his eyes and trying to work him out. 'How is that?'

'You are legendary around here, Mr Spooks,' Flint said respectfully. 'That's all Charlie Greech has been chirping about recently. He seems deadly serious on getting rid of you.'

'Yeah, Charlie and I go a long way back,' Killian admitted. 'I'd like to get out of here and meet him again to show my appreciation. Such a nice guy.' Killian half smiled.

'I can see by your face,' Flint said looking at the welts on his skin. 'He must really like you.'

Killian smiled, but even that hurt.

'Our next move is to get to that window before it disappears,' Zoot announced urgently. 'We don't know how long it will be there.'

'Well, I'll leave you two gentlemen to sort that and get back to your lives. And I'll find my way back to mine, bye.' Flint said, and with that, was gone.

'Uh... bye,' Killian said, 'and thanks.' But he was waving to thin air.

'Wow, he can move fast for an older guy. I don't see him anywhere,' Zoot gasped.

'Nice guy though.' Killian said, still pondering on the fire show that just happened. Then Zoot pulled him back to the urgency of their situation.

'Killian, we'd better go,' Zoot piped up. 'I'm sorry Greech did that to your face. It's my fault for not getting us out through that window.'

Killian touched his face; it was quite sore. Also, his eye was quite puffy with the bruise starting to form. 'That was not your fault, Zoot. Don't blame yourself. That fucker did a number on me all right. Forget that for now, we've got to get out of here. I don't want Charlie catching up with us. And I definitely don't want to spend any more time in that jail,' Killian said.

'Hopefully they won't discover we've gone for a while,' Zoot said. 'His two guards won't be shouting out a warning, that's for sure. And he won't find them, no matter how hard he tries,' Zoot uttered, as he looked at the two scorch marks on the floor.

'Hold on, before I go, I have to get my wand,' Killian remembered with urgency. 'I've felt so vulnerable without it. I've never been separated from it before.' He opened the box on the desk and gazed lovingly at the silver pen. He picked it up, placed it in his pocket and gently patted the small bulge. Now he felt whole again.

'We have to go, Killian.'

'Right, let's get outside and see what's waiting for us.' Zoot just nodded in compliance and they gently pushed open the door to leave.

# Chapter 10
# The Bridge

Killian and Zoot couldn't see Flint anywhere when they finally opened the door and stepped onto the porch; he'd long gone. There were no guards or anyone in the immediate area.

'Wow, he didn't waste any time, did he?' Zoot said.

'I don't blame him, do you?' Killian replied and looked out over the town square. It was quiet and Killian was always nervous when that happened. 'Where is everyone?'

'It's weird,' Zoot agreed 'Something is going on or we'd be dead by now.'

Killian guessed that Charlie Greech must have been rallying his troops after being called away from killing him on the spot. 'I don't like this,' Killian said biting his bottom lip.

'This is a good chance to make our escape and find that window.' Zoot perked up.

'Things are rarely that easy Zoot, as you well know,' Killian rasped. 'Shit.'

'What is it, Killian? What have you remembered?' Zoot said, looking deep into the wizard's eyes.

'We have to think why those guards came back,' Killian continued, with a slight shake of the head. 'What if Greech sent them to get one of us, to kill in front of his men? If that's the case then he'll be here soon wondering why they haven't returned,' Killian surmised. His face was aching and his hand was throbbing, too, where Greech had thrown the rock at him in the cave. He looked down. It was bruised and slightly swollen.

'Then we have to move right away,' Zoot said urgently.

'Agreed. Come on,' Killian replied. The two friends retraced their steps back to the site where the mirror hung, but it wasn't there any more. Neither were Charlie Greech or his men.

'This is not good,' Zoot complained, his head still hurting. 'We're stuck here now,' he said and he tensed at the thought. He felt sick. Was it the head wound making him nauseous, or the idea of being trapped here forever?

'Great,' Killian muttered quietly under his breath.

'What now?' Zoot asked and looked blankly at his friend. But, if he was honest with himself, Killian didn't appear too confident about anything right now. He looked defeated. Zoot waited for him to speak and when he finally did, Zoot wished he hadn't.

'I don't know. I honestly don't,' Killian admitted and sat on a rock. 'Where the hell is it?' he searched his mind for answers and closed his eyes in concentration. Everything was so quiet and peaceful. If it weren't for the fact that Killian knew this world inside and out, he would have thought it a nice place to relax. But he also knew that any minute now, this whole world could be turned upside down. It may have been dark and serene, but they were in the land of the dead and evil spilt out of every shadow.

'Ah, my phone,' he remembered. With everything that had gone on and the knocks to his head, he'd forgotten about the GPS. He was thinking more clearly.

'Er, Killian,' Zoot piped up, but the wizard was dipping into his pocket for his mobile. '*Killian!*' Zoot shrieked. This seemed to break the wizard's concentration.

'What?' Killian snapped back. 'What do you want, Zoot? I'm trying to…' Killian stopped and looked. 'Oh shit. When… how did that happen?' Killian asked. Zoot just shook his head. There was a bridge in the middle of a lake, neither of which were there earlier. The whole apparition was lit throughout with lighted torches that cut through the depressive darkness like beacons. Killian understood that things could change rapidly here. He also seemed to recognise its appearance because his face changed from a grimace to a broad smile.

'What is it, Killian?' Zoot pressed urgently. 'Do you know anything about that?' he asked, pointing to the apparition. Just then their worst fears were recognised. From across the way, they heard the familiar echo of Charlie Greech's voice in a full high-pitched rant. He sounded angry and didn't seem that far away.

'Oh, God,' Zoot gulped. 'We've got to go.'

'Come on, Zoot, we have to get to the bridge,' Killian screamed. 'That's a sign.'

'What… no, we have to get away from here,' Zoot responded.

'And go where? Even if you morphed into a bird or something — where would we go?' Killian asked. 'No, that bridge must mean something. I'm going that way.' He jabbed his finger in the direction of the apparition.

'Just follow me to the bridge,' he snapped angrily. 'It's our only chance.'

'No. I'm not going. We have to try and find some other way to get out of here,' Zoot pleaded, 'maybe hide in the hills?'

'Please trust me on this and don't ask questions, Zoot. Let's get to the bridge and quickly. Charlie will find us eventually and you know how that ends,' Killian insisted, and seemed fired up.

'He'll only follow us over there,' Zoot sighed. 'We'll be trapped.' But Killian wasn't listening any more. He was already sprinting towards the lake. 'Killian,' Zoot called after him. 'Killian.'

'Just shut up and follow me if you want to live,' Killian shouted back and dashed across the ground. Zoot gave out a huff and reluctantly ran after his friend. Both of them sped across the open ground towards the lake with the bridge perched upon it. Behind them was Charlie Greech, leading his whole zombie army after them. Hundreds of scavengers scurried along the ground, silent and deadly.

'What good is the bridge going to make?' Zoot complained, still not convinced.

'For fuck's sake, just trust me on this one.' Killian was losing his patience. The whole area around them was bathed in shadows of deep blues and sombre greys from the glow of the bridge's burning stakes. As they approached, they saw that the water that pooled around the bridge's structure appeared calm and smooth. It was as flat and as black as a large coin, but glossy-black in colour.

The bridge itself was a wooden structure and beautifully curved in the middle with a sweeping arch. It had wide boards as a base, and upright struts connected to a continuous handrail. Also, the burning stakes were set in segments along its length and illuminated the bridge, reflecting against the water's dark surface. The whole structure was set inside the perimeter of the lake. There were about two metres of water at each end between the bridge and the bank. And Killian realised this right away and immediately warned Zoot.

'Don't touch the water as you get to the bridge, jump over it,' Killian shouted as he ran and leapt over the gap and landed on the wooden deck. He kept on going though and didn't stop until he was at the apex. Zoot jumped as he'd been told and eventually caught up with Killian. They stood, both surveying the perimeter, both panting wildly, mouths open, gasping for air.

'What now?' Zoot said sucking in air through his teeth. 'I hope I don't live to regret this,' he said almost breathless.

'Zoot… do you trust me?' Killian asked simply, and when Zoot went to say something, he put his hand up in front of the monk's face. 'Do-you-trust-me?' Killian repeated. Zoot didn't answer at first. Killian waited and Zoot nodded.

'Okay, then,' Killian spoke. 'Thank you, that's all I ask.'

'What do we do now?' Zoot spoke calmly as his breath returned.

'We wait,' Killian said simply, 'that's all we can do.'

'Wait? Okay.' Zoot concentrated his eyes on the advancing enemy and swallowed hard. They could see them come into view in the distance. There were way too many to try and fight their way out of this one. And anyway — where would they go if they did?

But Zoot then he stopped panicking. He stared, almost in a hypnotic trance. What was going on?

Instead of the bridge being breached, meaning sudden death for both of them — nothing happened. The scavengers came from everywhere and surrounded them, but stayed put. Maybe they were waiting for instructions from their commander? Zoot didn't know. He suddenly felt safer. But Killian did say to trust him. And Zoot realised that of all the times he'd known the wizard, he hadn't let him down... not once.

Why aren't they attacking? Zoot rolled the thought through his mind. He'd noticed that they were standing well away from the bridge and the water's edge. Maybe they don't like washing, he mused. He was baffled and leaned over to rest his elbows on the handrail. He peered down into the blackness of the water and shifted uncomfortably.

There were things in the lake. He didn't know what they were, but there was movement under the surface. He looked back at Killian who didn't look as worried; he actually appeared relaxed. Zoot narrowed his eyes in puzzlement.

'What is happening?' Zoot quizzed.

'We're safe for the moment. Charlie and his cronies won't come any nearer this place,' Killian said with confidence. Zoot looked at Charlie Greech's zombie soldiers. They each had the same vacant look on their faces he'd seen every time he'd come into contact with them. Some were in worse shape than others, with decayed and mottled skin and some missing limbs.

'Why? What's so special about this place?' Zoot pestered.

'Because this is the Lake of Eternal Darkness,' Killian explained knowingly.

'What does that even mean? Do you make these things up? *The Lake of Eternal Darkness*,' Zoot said in his most dramatic voice, and used his arms for visual effect. 'It can't kill them — they're already dead — so what are they scared of?'

Killian looked at his friend incredulously. 'No, it can't kill them, obviously, but it can send them to their eternal nothingness. They have some kind of existence right now, here in this shitty world. But if there were a chance of them falling into that,' and he pointed to the lake, 'then their puny lives would cease to exist completely. They'd have nothing… and no one wants a nothing existence — not even a scavenger,' Killian said.

'How did you know about this? I didn't, and I've spent quite a bit of time here too,' Zoot said. He sounded quite annoyed.

'I'm a wizard and we have certain feelings about places like this. Call it wizard's intuition.' Killian explained.

'Wizard's intuition,' Zoot mumbled in a whisper.

Killian stopped for a moment and gave him a look of distaste. He must have heard his remark. 'It doesn't matter that you haven't heard of this place. But what it does do is buy us time. Time to try and work out where the window is and try and figure a way out of this.'

The troops stood at the perimeter of the lake. There wasn't any way of escaping.

'Why don't they simply attack us with their weapons?' Zoot asked, and then the thought of being a sitting duck made him cringe.

'Because none of them will chance it,' Killian explained. 'They may be a brainless, bunch of zombies, but if one spear hits the water, that could upset the spirits. And they don't want the spirits turning on them.'

'So we're safe?' Zoot added with confidence.

'I don't know for how long though,' Killian admitted, and then he pointed Zoot in the direction of a single scavenger. He'd broken the ranks and walked along to the edge of the water. The others looked on; their expressions were as blank as an empty canvas.

This one particular figure stooped down and held its bony face just centimetres from the surface of the water. It grinned, revealing a mouthful of broken blackened teeth. Killian picked up on its confidence and stared intensely. The next moment, and as fast as a slingshot, two skeletal arms burst through from below and gripped the unsuspecting scavenger around its neck. It tried to pull away, but the arms were locked on. The scavenger didn't stand a chance and was instantly dragged into the murky black liquid. The others saw this and shuffled backwards. The creature made an ear-piercing shriek just before it was pulled under. There were mutterings from within the ranks. The water sloshed about for a couple of seconds and quickly returned to its calm, smooth exterior once more. Killian and Zoot looked on in deadly silence.

Suddenly a line of the dead parted as Charlie Greech pushed his way through the throng and walked to one end of the bridge. He smiled as he gazed into Killian's eyes.

'No way out of this one, Spooky! Come over here and we can talk.'

# Chapter 11
## No Escape

Killian looked at his nemesis with contempt and ignored the name-calling — there was no point in quibbling any more. If he thought about it, he didn't see any way out of this dire situation. He didn't tell Zoot how he felt — his monk friend was stressed enough. But he'd called Zoot here... and ironically it was to save his own life. But now they might both die and Killian felt bad enough. He had to face the full situation he'd put himself in.

If the demons under the water didn't get them, then the demons above the water would. How could he bluff his way out of this one? There must be a way, he thought. Think, Killian, think.

'Hey, Greech. I thought you were in the middle of something — you know, the way you rushed off earlier?' Killian probed.

Charlie Greech gave out a huge, false chuckle. 'No. That was a false alarm, Spooky. But I'm sure that someone will try and take my throne at some point. That will be no concern of yours. You'll already be crushed beyond recognition long before then,' he said, still sniggering, the mottled skin on his cheeks glistening from the yellow flames of the fire. 'Oh, by the way, how is your eye? That looks angry. Did someone smack you for being so fucking stupid?' Greech burst out into another fit of false laughter.

Killian mulled things over for a second. 'If you think you can finish the job, then why don't you come over here?' Killian said, extending an invitation. 'I mean, I'm wide open. No risk to you at all. Are you scared, little one?'

'Killian,' Zoot interrupted urgently, but trying to keep his voice low. 'Are you nuts? We're in a sketchy situation as it is.' Zoot couldn't believe what he was hearing.

'Just go with it,' Killian said out of the corner of his mouth. He quickly noticed Charlie Greech's agitation and smiled back at him. 'Oh. You are afraid, aren't you?' Killian spoke with a condescending tone and knew he had him rattled. 'You don't like it when your opponent is free to fight back. You'd rather beat them when they're bound and defenceless? You're a coward, Greechy boy,' Killian declared, making sure to push all of his buttons and vent his anger at the same time. Charlie Greech's eyes flared and Killian could see him grinding his rotten, unsightly teeth — he had him. 'Why don't you send one of your loyal followers to come and grab me? Hold on, one was just swallowed up by the lake, wasn't it? Aw,' he said, 'that's a real shame.' Charlie Greech stood in front of his vast band of scavengers. They were still and silent like sheep herded in a pen.

'Don't push your luck, Killian,' Zoot hissed. It was true, Killian was enjoying this a bit too much. Charlie Greech was ready to explode, like a rocket primed in a fireworks display. His face was a picture of anger and he was more or less bouncing up and down on the spot.

'I'll rip your fucking head off, you freaking wizard bastard,' Greech howled, his face contorted in a myriad of shapes. 'You poor excuse for a fucking sorcerer. I'll kill you and your friend. I'll kill fucking everyone,' he ranted filled with frustration. 'I'll-I'll, tear you a new one, you...'

Zoot glanced at Killian and rolled his eyes. 'I think you've upset him, Killian — the language on that guy,' Zoot said, but he was amused too.

Killian nodded in acknowledgement. 'Maybe too much, but while he's seeing red, he's not thinking clearly and that's an advantage,' Killian explained, 'and we need all the time we can get to figure something out.' Killian dipped into his pocket and glanced at the screen, but it wouldn't work in the dead zone in which they were situated.

'Damn,' Killian hissed while Charlie was still screaming in the background.

'What is it?' Zoot asked.

'I can't find the window with my phone in this area. It's like we're in some sort of bubble,' Killian assumed and put his phone away. Finally, all the ranting stopped and Charlie stood breathless on the bank. Then something really strange happened that took everyone by surprise. The window, which had brought both of them, appeared out of nowhere — right on top of the lake. Its mirrored effect shimmered above the light of the flames.

'Oh my God,' Zoot gushed. 'Oh my God,' he repeated, his hopes returning tenfold. Killian couldn't believe it either. Charlie Greech was even more agitated now. He thought he finally had Killian. But, with this window appearing again, his chances were slipping away. Greech knew he couldn't use it because his powers were weak on the other side. And he didn't want the wizard to return home. He was thinking of some way of destroying it.

'How are we going to get to that?' Killian said. It was hovering over the lake.

'It's perfect. We can fly over there.' Zoot said, but Killian wasn't listening. He was realising the dangers of the portal. The window appeared as a bright, shimmering image in the centre of the lake.

It was too close to the bridge for Charlie Greech and his followers to touch. And it was just out of reach for Killian and Zoot. The other problem was that it was only a matter of centimetres from the surface of the water too. It was in the most dangerous position for the monk and wizard to get to it. It was as if someone was toying with them.

'Shit,' Killian grimaced.

'What?' Zoot asked, the concern showing on his face. 'It's our escape route. Let's go.'

'Yeah, but what if the ghouls in this lake see it and they decide that they want to enter our world too?' Killian said. 'We have to climb through and seal it so that no one else can enter. 'Hey Greech. Are you sure that you are not in control of that thing?' Killian called out, 'it seems to follow you like a bad smell.'

'Yeah, I wish it did,' he replied honestly for once. 'Like I told you before — it just appeared and I went through to your world. It comes and goes as it wants. I have no control over it, but it won't matter to you anyway. You're stuck here, my friend.'

'What do you mean?' Killian shouted back.

'Because once those monsters from the lake see it, they'll climb through — I'm sure you've already thought of that? And that would leave you to me and your world to them!' Charlie Greech was in

115

his element. No matter which way this went, he was going to win regardless.

'That's not going to happen,' Killian reacted, 'not if I can help it.'

'I've got to change before it shuts, Killian,' Zoot said. 'It's too far for us to reach.'

'That won't happen,' Killian said and his expression was grave. 'I didn't tell you about our powers with this bridge. There's more grave news, my friend.'

'What do you mean?' Zoot looked puzzled and scared. 'We haven't time for this, Killian.'

'You can't shape shift on the bridge,' Killian spoke up. 'It won't let you use your powers. Or anyone else's powers, come to that, even mine. Greech might have won this time.' Killian sighed. He looked over at the leader of the scavengers. Charlie Greech just grinned back at him with his arms folded over his chest. Just waiting for his chance.

Zoot looked as though he was contorted in pain. He was doubled over and the strain on his face was immense.

'What are you doing, man? You look fucking constipated,' Killian said, his eyebrows arched.

'I'm trying to change into a large bird so I can fly us out of here,' Zoot confessed, 'but it's not working.'

'Well, unless you're willing to leave a large brown deposit on the bridge, I can't see you doing much else any time soon. I told you. This bridge won't let you change.' Killian was serious.

'You're making jokes at a time like this. You're nuts, Killian,' Zoot raged. 'I don't want to die here.' Zoot was upset and Killian couldn't do much to reassure him.

'Yeah, well neither do I. So, stop pouting and help me figure this out, will you?' Killian suggested. They looked at the shimmering escape route and then back at the army of morons waiting for them. Charlie Greech broke their concentration.

'Come on over here, Spooky and take what's coming to you,' Charlie Greech piped up. Suddenly, there was a huge eruption of sound that boomed across the land. It was so loud, in fact, that the bridge shuddered and the water in the lake rippled into a choppy sea.

Killian and Zoot had to grab hold of the handrail just to steady themselves and stay upright. A few unlucky scavengers, who were standing a bit too close to the lake, toppled over and fell in. Once they were under the water, a multitude of hands grabbed them. It only took a matter of seconds before they were all dragged to the bottom. Then came another boom and added to that an eruption of flames shot across the sky.

'What the fuck was that?' Killian hissed. 'This isn't right.'

'Thunder perhaps?' Zoot assumed.

'Not in this world,' Killian assured him. Soon another eruption and more fire penetrated the dark world and the scavengers began to scatter, even on hearing the outburst of protests from their master.

'You fucking cowards, get back here. Come back, you mangy shits,' Charlie Greech bellowed, but his army evaporated into the darkness. Killian looked on in bewilderment. What had caused such fear and devastation? He looked for an answer in the darkness but there was nothing. When Charlie Greech realised, he was now all alone, he peered over at Killian and gave him a look of disgust.

'This is not the end, Spooky,' he said, before he scampered off too, shouting obscenities in his wake. Killian and Zoot immediately made their way off the bridge. They were lucky; the window was still in the same position, untouched.

'What just happened?' Zoot asked.

'Search me,' Killian retorted, 'but whatever it was has helped us big time. We've got to make the most of it and get through that window right away.' They were about to move off.

'Yep, you'd better get a move on.' The familiar voice of Flint sounded behind them. Killian spun round and the shock on his face was priceless.

'You did that?' Killian said with a gasp. 'The flames I understand, but how did you create such huge sound?' Killian asked — filled with curiosity.

'Just a little trick I've developed, which normally gets me out of trouble. They overpowered me last time, so I couldn't use the thunder. This time I had the advantage. I could see you needed help so I thought one good turn deserved another. You broke me out of prison and so we're square now,' Flint explained.

'Sounds good to me, thank you,' Killian said in appreciation. 'I hope we meet again some time, Flint.' Killian offered a handshake and was duly reciprocated. 'If you don't mind me asking — what are you?'

'I'm flint and I'm a fire spirit,' Flint said nonchalantly.

'Cool,' Killian grinned.

'Hot actually,' Flint responded.

'Your jokes are worse than Killian's,' Zoot added, 'and I thank you from the bottom of my heart, Flint,' Zoot said and shook hands, just before he changed into a griffin.

'Wow, that's quite cool too.' Flint seemed impressed. 'Haven't seen one of those… ever,' he said smiling.

'Thank you again,' Killian added, with warmth. 'If you ever need a hand with something, don't hesitate to contact me.'

'I may take you up on that some time. Safe journey and take it easy,' Flint said, as Killian climbed onto the back of the griffin and they flew straight into the void. Killian uttered a spell as they crossed over the rim, which instantly sealed the void so no one else could enter. And soon, they were through to the other side. First, the light hurt their eyes, and the heat of summer followed. It was a welcome change to the cold, bleak world of the dead. And they were safe again for the time being…

# Chapter 12
## A Stray

Zoot was immediately blinded by the brilliant sunlight and crash-landed into a mound of grass. The two of them were tangled up on a grassy knoll.

'Aaaargh, great landing, Zoot,' Killian complained, spitting turf out of his mouth.

'Oowwww,' was all that Zoot could reply. Killian pushed the fast-disappearing bird off his chest. Zoot slumped onto his back, fully changed back into his monk persona. They looked a sight — Killian with his eye swollen and slowly turning black, followed by a bruise on his jaw and a mark on his hand; Zoot, with his robe covered in bloodstains from the beast in the cave. He also had many bruises that covered his naked body, from various encounters in the last few days. They lay there for a moment to take in the peace and calm.

'It's great to be back. Now put something on, for Christ's sake,' Killian sighed as he looked up at the blue expanse. 'It felt like we were in that dark, freaking place for an age.'

'I ache all over,' Zoot whimpered. 'I need tea.' He scrambled in the bushes where he found his clean robe. (He tried to keep spares for obvious reasons.)

'Yeah, me too — not the tea, but the aching all over bit,' Killian admitted. 'Well, we have been through kind of a lot in the dark world and only a few hours have passed.'

'Anyway, I've got to get back home — I've got a few things I have to sort out,' Zoot remembered, reeling things off in his mind.

Killian eventually got to his feet and stretched his back. 'Yeah, of course. Thanks for everything, Zoot, and as usual you've been amazing,' Killian praised. 'I can't believe that Charlie Greech was waiting there for me all this time. I'm not going back there in a hurry.'

'Hey, we'll catch up soon, eh?' Zoot grinned. 'Hey, hold on…' Zoot was about to leave when he spotted something.

'What is it, Zoot?' Killian asked, still reeling from their experience.

'There's something there, behind you, Killian,' Zoot said and peered past Killian's shoulder.

'Yeah. Right. Good one, Zoot. I know I've got to close that window. I've already sealed the other end,' Killian chuckled. 'Let's leave the jokes for another time, eh? It's been a long…' Killian stopped talking when he heard a long, deep growl. 'Oh shit,' he said.

When he turned around, he saw the shimmering image of the window was still there, but in the bushes below it, there was something else, something moving, disturbing the undergrowth. Both of them tensed, waiting for whatever it was to appear.

Killian felt in his pocket and pulled out his pen; it immediately changed from a silver writing instrument into a long, black wand, lit at the tip.

Zoot stood parallel to Killian's shoulder. 'What do you suppose it is?' Zoot spoke softly, not taking his eyes from the trembling bushes. 'They couldn't have followed us through, could they?' he gulped.

'I don't want it to be them, but we'd best be prepared to fight, just in case it is,' Killian said with eyes wide. 'Can you morph into something to help me?' Killian questioned.

'I-I don't think I can.' Zoot trembled.

Killian looked shocked. 'Why not?' Killian appeared pale.

'I'm too weak now. I've changed so many times today that it's taken its toll,' he admitted. 'I need to regenerate.'

'Really? Jesus Christ,' Killian rasped. 'I understand. Don't worry, I've got this,' Killian didn't sound confident.

'Sorry, Killian,' Zoot uttered.

'Don't sweat it. You've done all you can. Now it's my turn.' Killian straightened up and appeared taller. 'Call it,' Killian asked.

'Come out of there,' Zoot cried. The shuffling stopped. 'You heard me. Come and face us, you coward,' he said. Soon, the reeds parted and out came a short, black figure. It was a mangled, mess, definitely not human. This thing had a glossy exterior, but no real distinguishing features. It appeared to have two hind legs, but its upper body was hunched over as if it had been in a car accident. Killian could make out two eyes and it had two arms, which were tucked into its sides.

The wizard didn't waste time and let loose with a blast from his wand. The creature, though, was too quick and easily sidestepped the shot. The lightning bolt flew over its head and struck a tree directly behind it. The magical force tore a hole through it, the size of a football.

'Fuck it, I missed,' Killian groaned and aimed again, unaware that the beast was nearly on him.

'Look out,' Zoot screamed and wrenched Killian to one side. They tumbled backwards onto the ground with Killian slightly dazed.

'What are you doing?' he screamed until he saw the creature had landed next to them and was gathering itself on the ground. 'You saved me,' Killian responded and got to his feet in double-quick time.

'Shut up and fire again,' Zoot bellowed. Then Killian realised that the creature was already standing. He lifted his wand to aim, but the monster smacked it out of his hand. Killian only had moments but managed to mutter a spell under his breath. He quickly raised his hands and sent a force that slammed into the ugly creature's mid-section. It went tumbling backwards along the ground and ended up upside down. It stopped by a tree trunk with its legs in the air.

'Good work, Killian, now zap it again,' Zoot praised, 'quickly before it can get up.'

'Where's my wand?' Killian was in turmoil.

'Killian, he's coming again,' Zoot screamed, but the wizard was already scrambling in the grass for his wand. The monster charged at him and smacked into his side. Killian went sprawling onto the grass clutching his hip.

'Fu-ck, that hurt,' he screamed. The impact knocked the wind out of his lungs and left him gasping for air. The demon climbed on top of the stricken wizard and gripped him around the throat. It began to slowly throttle him. Killian's face went blue and his eyes began to bulge out of his head. Zoot didn't know what to do. He was still weak.

Killian could see the deep whites of the monster's eyes and he could feel his own life slowly draining away. As he gasped for air, he could see the creature's face right next to his. It didn't have a nose, but its mouth was wide and stank to high heaven. He could see deep inside its throat. The teeth were sharp enough to tear a cow to shreds. Soon, Killian's head pounded like a giant drum and nothing seemed to matter any more.

The beast was strong. Killian's vision blurred and the fiend's image became ghosted and grainy. Pictures flashed across the wizard's vision — Penny, his girlfriend, smiling, but soon turning to tears. She was all in black now, standing over a headstone, but even if it was his, he didn't care. His eyes eventually lost focus and he felt so light, like a soap bubble floating to the sky. He found that he didn't need to breathe at all. It was a nice feeling, the sensation of emptiness. All his troubles were leaving him, like dust in a gentle breeze. Soon his sight turned to eventual blackness.

The bear attacked the monster instantly. It was easily twice the alien's size and three-times as powerful. It grabbed the creature by its head and in one quick movement ripped it completely off. The sound of its neck being snapped echoed through the trees. Black liquid sprayed from the neck wound as the torso stopped moving and slumped on top of Killian's body. Zoot instantly tossed the head over his shoulder and it went flying into the portal, and was swallowed up in a second. Zoot then lifted the beast off his friend and fed that into the portal too. It digested the headless, contorted body like branches in a wood chipper. It disappeared in seconds and so, too, did the window. In a flash, everything was gone.

Zoot's body soon restored to his original form. He urgently dropped to his knees and felt Killian's neck for a pulse. It was there, but very weak. Now the pressure was lifted from Killian's throat, he could breathe again. Zoot saw his stomach rise and fall and in the next instant, there was a barrage of choking and coughing — the wizard was back. Killian sucked in air hungrily, as if he'd never breathed it before. His face was as red as a newly painted fence. He couldn't talk for a while and just lay there panting and sounded like an old locomotive. The redness faded eventually and his natural colour returned to his cheeks and he tried to swallow. He gulped and groaned, but calmed down and soon breathed naturally again. He looked at his friend and couldn't speak. Finally, his voice returned in a croak.

'Wh-at the fu-ck was that?' Killian said, his voice hoarse.

'Even close to death you use bad language,' Zoot scolded.

'Hold on,' Killian whispered in a husky tone. 'What happened, Zoot? I don't remember anything,' he said, and slowly pushed himself up onto his bum.

'It had you and almost to the point of death. I couldn't let it take you, my friend,' Zoot said sincerely. He took a few seconds and then added, 'I thought that was it. I did think you were a gonna, but I managed to change into a bear with what was left of my strength,' he admitted.

'Thank you, Zoot. I can't thank you enough. You went to the dark world to help me and risked your own life again and again,' Killian was filled with admiration for his friend. 'And now you've saved my life again.'

'Yeah, if you put it like that,' Zoot mused.

'I think I love you, Zoot,' Killian said, and stared deeply into Zoot's eyes.

'What?' Zoot was feeling uncomfortable.

'I want to kiss you,' Killian leaned in.

'Nooo,' Zoot retorted and looked disgusted.

'Come on, let me kiss you — kiss you and kiss you again,' Killian grinned.

Zoot pulled away and then saw his friend laughing. 'You... bastard,' Zoot cursed, realising that Killian was pulling his leg.

'Z-O-O-T... you just swore. Monks are not supposed to swear. What will all the other monks think?' Killian's face was semi-serious.

'Shut up and by the way... bastard is not a swear word,' Zoot said, trying to get out of it.

'I think you'll find it is,' Killian teased.

'I've had enough of this. I'm going home,' he said, and Killian just fell about laughing.

'I'm sorry, mate. I just couldn't resist,' Killian said playfully. 'I think we've had enough excitement for one day.'

'Yeah, I know what you mean. I have to go now,' Zoot said, 'I'm exhausted.

'But seriously, man — thank you for everything. And I mean everything.' Killian said, sincerely this time.

'That's no problem, Killian. If I've ever needed help you've always been there for me,' Zoot responded.

'Okay, catch you later, friend,' Killian added.

'You coming?' his friend asked.

'I'm just going to sit here for a while to catch my breath,' Killian told him and Zoot left. It was getting late. Killian was stiff. His eye throbbed, he had a headache and he ached in places that he didn't think possible. He got up with a long groan. A glow caught his attention in the grass and he reached for it. It was his homing stone, and he kissed it, and immediately winced when it touched his sore lip. They were getting ready to close the park and he strolled past the clock tower, which was in the middle of the duck pond. The time was eight-thirty. It had only been a matter of four or five hours since he'd been gone. It felt like much, much, longer than that. He was hungry and thirsty. He wasn't going to the pub again and decided to head home. He'd have something to eat and take a shower. Then put some ice on his face and relax for the evening; he deserved it. Fighting monsters and winding up his friend was exhausting. Unfortunately, it's what wizards had to do sometimes, but the drama was over for now. He thought of Charlie Greech and wondered if he'd ever meet him again. Killian shuddered and made his way home. Tomorrow he had a thief to catch.

# Chapter 13:
# Back to reality

By the time Killian walked back to his flat, it was around the nine o'clock mark. The night air was cool on his face and felt pleasant, taking away some of the pain. He waited outside his building apartment for a few minutes and just breathed in. He was tired and everything seemed to ache, especially his face; he could thank Charlie Greech for that. When he climbed the stairs to his office, he saw a note stuck to the glass-panelled door. He peeled it off and recognised the handwriting immediately — it was his girlfriend, Penny. Killian winced, not in pain, but at the thought of Penny coming over and him not being there. He couldn't remember if he'd promised her a night out or something. She was probably really mad at him, he assumed. He read the note.

*Hi Killian*

*I dropped by and obviously you're not here. Phone me to let me know you're okay.*

*Penny xxx.*

Killian smiled as he unlocked the door and let himself in. It had been a long day and so much had happened in such a short space of time, in the mortal world. Initially, he'd gone out to find the phantom thief and sort that case out for Chief Inspector Daniel Hathaway. But Killian hadn't expected to veer away from that and end up in the dark world. He also hadn't expected to come face to face again with Charlie Greech and battle a bloody swamp dog. And he hadn't expected to involve his monk friend, Zoot. Zoot had taken a massive risk by just stepping through the mirror. Both of them stuck on the Lake of Eternal Darkness. And, of course, there was the charismatic, character, Flint the fire spirit — what an amazing guy.

Killian shook his head and tried to clear the thoughts of the last few hours out of his mind. He took a long, soapy shower — the hot water felt as though it was healing as well as cleaning his bruised body. When he finished, he dried and put on some fresh clothes. He was drained of energy and the hot water had taken his last ounce of strength. He found some ice cubes in his freezer, wrapped them in a cloth and applied it to his eye. The icepack got most of the swelling down, but there was no hiding the fact that a black eye was emerging.

His order from the Chinese takeaway (a couple of doors from his apartment) came while he was drinking his coffee. He paid the guy and ate it in a matter of minutes. He was hungry — fighting evil will do that to you. He sat for a while again pondering all that had happened to him and other adventures that he'd been involved in in the past. He thought to himself that he'd have to write it all down one day. Write a novel, he smiled… never going to happen — he'd failed English in high school, in fact, he hated English.

'This job is certainly interesting though,' he said. He drained his coffee cup and then remembered he had to phone Penny. He'd been putting it off and didn't know why. Killian finally grabbed the phone in his office. It was an old push-button type (he didn't own a normal mobile phone — the one he hid only worked on a supernatural level and Penny didn't know about that one). It didn't take long for Penny to answer.

'Hi, babe,' he said in a soft tone, 'what's up?' as if he didn't know.

'Hi yourself.' She sounded annoyed. 'Are you okay? Why didn't you call me earlier? I was worried. Why don't you own a mobile? Killian, you need to keep in touch,' she ranted.

'Wow. Slow down,' he said, trying to cut in, 'I was busy and couldn't. Sorry if I worried you. I didn't mean to, Penny, honestly.' As he spoke his face ached, especially his black eye. He wasn't going to tell her about that; she'd only worry even more about him. But he obviously couldn't hide it forever from her. He added, 'Look, I don't want a mobile. Those things are a pain in the arse. Everybody wants you all the time and there's no escape. I haven't time for that,' he complained. 'I don't want one.'

'Okay, okay, I get it. You want to stay in the last century, fine,' she said and stopped. There was a pause and both of them took a breath from the heated conversation to calm down. So, eventually, Penny spoke up. 'Are you coming over tonight? We don't seem to have time for each other these days.'

Killian realised he'd been neglecting her recently. He knew he'd been distant. It was the job. It was all-consuming, but there again she knew that too because she gave him the cases. Sometimes a job could take him away for days at a time. Sometimes he didn't even know if he'd return.

'Babe…' Killian said softly on the other end of the line, 'about tonight…' he said in a gentle tone. He didn't remember if they'd made a date — he was just testing the water in case they had made plans. With everything that had gone on, he simply couldn't remember. His inkling was realised when she answered.

'You're not coming, are you?' she realised and suddenly went quiet. He could picture her pressing her luscious red lips together and staring blankly at the wall with those beautiful, azure eyes. She always looked even more beautiful when she was upset. He had to make it up to her somehow. If he didn't, she might grow tired of him and if he was honest with himself, he couldn't live without her. She could have the pick of the bunch, but chose him.

'It's been a very difficult day and I'm really tired, Penny. I'm sorry. I'll make it up to you — I will, honest. It's just, you know the cases I work on aren't your normal run of the mill police situations,' Killian assured her. 'Sometimes other things are involved. You know that first hand with the spirit jumper problem we had a while ago.'

She did remember because she was one of the victims of that case. She sat back on her sofa and remembered the horrors of that time, which came back in a flash of bad images.

'Being a wizard has its problems,' he admitted, 'and things run over sometimes. If you want me to come over now, I will,' he said hoping that she wouldn't. He could hear her taking a long, deep breath on the line.

'F-i-n-e,' she relented, extending the word as far as she could. He knew she was okay with it. She was like that. That was what he loved about her. 'I know some of the things you have to deal with.'

'Do you forgive me, my sweet, sexy girl?' he asked, his voice sickly.

'Oh, shut up, you idiot,' she relented and smiled, because that was what she liked about him — his nonsense phrases and general tomfoolery.

'Are we okay?'

'Yes… I suppose so, you dick,' she said.

'Charming. Miss White, the things you come out with sometimes really shock me,' Killian replied with a giggle.

'Don't be flippant, Killian,' she countered with a superior pitch. 'Oh, by the way, did you get the file I put by your office door? Also, have you made any progress with the pickpocket case at the train station?

Hathaway is pressing me for results on that one.' She groaned. Killian laughed out loud at the end of the line. 'What are you laughing at?' she asked, intrigued, wrinkling her nose, pressing her lips together.

'Oh, only the way the conversation has gone from romance… to straight into a work scenario,' he mused. 'Is that all I am to you, a case solver and a sex toy for your enjoyment,' Killian said, perking up.

'Don't detract from the conversation, Killian,' Penny said, 'and yes that is all you are to me.'

If he was honest with himself, he'd forgotten to tell her about the guy at the station. Well, a lot had gone on in between. He'd have to give her an update when he had more to go on.

'I haven't got anything yet, Penny. I have a lead and I'll get onto it straight away in the morning. Just tell Hathaway that I'm making progress,' he said with confidence. 'I promise you I'll have something soon. I haven't seen a file,' he said rolling his eyes trying to remember. 'Maybe Glyn dropped it inside for me,' Killian assumed.

'What have you been up to all day then... wait, don't tell me. I don't think I want to know,' she said realising it could have been mind-blowing.

'Best you don't actually,' he commented, adding a yawn, but not meaning to. 'I will tell you the full story when we see each other next. There is a lot to talk about,' he said with another yawn.

'You do sound tired. I'll let you go then, as long as you promise me a meal out somewhere soon?' she reminded him. 'I miss you.'

'Of course I will. A meal and my charming personality.' He could feel her warm smile. 'I miss you, too. We will spend more time together soon,' he added. 'Goodnight my sweet vixen. What are you wearing, by the way? Is it that tight, little blue number… phwaaah?' He loved winding her up and she enjoyed the banter too.

'Good night, Killian, and get those dirty thoughts out of your mind… and yes,' Penny responded sharply and put the receiver down.

He held that picture of her in his mind for a few seconds, and when the purr of the disconnect tone rattled in his head, he snapped out of it. Killian dropped the phone on the cradle. He refocused on the poltergeist at the station.

'I need to trap that dude sooner rather than later and find out where he resides, but that's in the morning,' he said, with another yawn. He flipped off the light in his office and made his way back into the living room. He glanced at the coffee table and saw the file Penny was talking about, Glyn must have brought it in for me, he nodded. That's going to have to wait for now, I've too much on right now. He ran his index finger along the large bookcase and stopped at a book called *Poltergeists and how to trap them*. That was his reading matter before he went to sleep. How long he would stay awake was another problem.

Killian sat on the bed and trawled through the pages, looking for something he could work with.

The bed felt so comfortable and his body was sore and he needed rest.

'My problem is that he's already seen me and he's going to be on his guard,' he mumbled. From what he was wearing, Killian couldn't tell from what period in time he belonged to. The warlock came across something interesting called a "hot spot". He read on: "Poltergeists leave traces of themselves when they move around. These are known as hot spots. But as any supernatural being knows, a poltergeist is anything but hot. When a non-supernatural is confronted with a poltergeist situation, they can experience sub-zero temperatures when close. The hot spot is only a term used. It's a spiritual footprint that only lasts for a short while before it dissolves. Some spiritual beings such as ghosts and poltergeists leave ectoplasm (a gooey-type residue) while others leave an "essence trail". These traces are only visible to someone with supernatural senses: such as witches, vampires, werewolves and warlocks. The essence is easily picked up with a simple spell."

Killian continued to read on in his head and memorised the spell he'd have to use. So, he wouldn't have to try and chase this being, only follow it. The subject should have moved onto the next world, but something or someone had trapped him here. Right, he had something to work with; he could pick up the trail. Killian smiled as he clapped the book shut. Now he had an advantage. But following a poltergeist was one thing and trapping one was going to be a different experience. But he put that to the back of his mind and as he closed his eyes, sleep came easily.

# Chapter 14
## Young Fagin

Killian got up early the next morning. When he moved to get out of bed every muscle hurt. He reached in the bedside cabinet and grabbed a couple of painkillers. Once he'd taken them his mind was trained on only one thing. He had to catch and dispose of the poltergeist that was plaguing the train station. Things were tight and bills needed paying. He had to get this case done and dusted so that he could get paid and firstly pay his rent, which was looming.

It was another great start to the day, weather-wise. The sun was already climbing the blue expanse and shone into his apartment, bathing the mat in a block of yellow. The heat was also building. It was going to be another scorcher. Killian thought of his task for the day.

He'd already named the spirit Young Fagin from the character in the Charles Dickens novel, Oliver Twist. Thinking about it after the event, it seemed appropriate even though Fagin was actually the old guy who was the instigator in the book; he had the Artful Dodger to train up his young thieves, so Young Fagin it was going to be.

Killian understood that he had to keep himself hidden so the youngster didn't realise he was being watched. Friday morning's rush hour was the perfect time to monitor the culprit. Once he'd done that, Killian had to find the location of his lair and that was going to be the difficult part. A lot was pinned on the victim not realising that he was being monitored. If the poltergeist suspected that someone was watching him again, he would be virtually impossible to keep track of. Even if his subject left the ectoplasm residue behind, a spiritual being could literally disappear and send its pursuer on a wild goose chase.

Killian looked at himself in the mirror. The swelling on his mouth was down and only a yellowy bruise remained. His eye, though, was another thing. He'd caught most of it the night before with the ice pack. Now there was only the darkened colour on the lower lid that stood out. He sighed and walked out of the bathroom. He cooked himself some eggs on toast and a downed a coffee before he set about his business.

He pushed his scooter outside into the warmth of the summer's morning and promptly started it up. It purred like a mechanical kitten and looked amazing, sitting on its stand. The morning air was fresh and he drank it in. There hadn't been rain for a few weeks. On the news, there was already a mention of a hosepipe ban — this made Killian giggle, it never took long for that. Killian climbed on and pulled away, leaving a pungent smell of petrol fumes behind. The road was busy as usual at this time of morning and he was quite skilled at weaving in and out of the traffic. He enjoyed the fact that a bike could move freely along the road. He loved the feeling of chilled air buffering under his visor and cooling his hot cheeks. He looked at all the frustrated faces stuck in traffic. He didn't envy for one minute, owning a car. His powder blue Vespa was his pride and joy. He zoomed along until he got to the station car park. He saw lots of people carrying shoulder bags or dragging their wheeled briefcases. He sat on his bike for a while watching. It was a busy Friday.

'I hope I can catch you today kid,' he said from inside his helmet. Witnessing all the activity also made him feel so happy that he wasn't part of the rat race. All those people were going to their big city offices and pandering to their superiors. Probably hated being chained to their desks for eight to ten hours. Then they had to make their way home and start all over again on Monday. He enjoyed his own work just fine the way it was.

He snapped back to reality and focused on the job he had to do. He switched off his engine and wheeled his bike to a safe spot behind a small building outside the station entrance. There, he put his helmet inside the seat and set his usual spell, to make his Vespa invisible. (He always did this to protect his bike from thieves.) When that was complete, he took a quick look around to make sure that no one saw him, or that there were any CCTV cameras in the vicinity. Satisfied, he made his way inside the train station.

First thing was to find a good vantage point from which to monitor the station and not be seen by his target. He knew that there was an open-air café on the upper floor of the station, which overlooked the platform below. It was perfect for passengers to have a coffee and keep an eye on when their train was going to arrive, or to collect someone who disembarked.

He noticed one or two people were already poised with cup in hand, either reading a paper or eyes fixed on a phone screen. Killian bought a coffee and sat down on a chair right by the wrought iron handrail. He placed his cup on the small, round, stainless steel table. He dipped into his shoulder bag and drew out a pair of sunglasses. But these weren't just ordinary shades. They served two purposes. One was to keep out the sun's glare and the painful reflection from the silver surface of the table; and the second, they'd been specially prepared with an enchantment to expose supernatural activity. Killian had also bought a newspaper, in order not to look too suspicious. In this day and age, he didn't want to get picked up by security for appearing as a potential terrorist suspect, thereby alerting his thief and blowing the whole case.

The scene was set. Killian half glanced at the pages — apparently there was a new boy band sensation sweeping the country. He shook his head in dismissal. He quickly turned the page, already annoyed at the waste of print. He took a quick look around, sweeping with the spirit gauge of the visor; nothing yet.

He felt like a character in a detective novel and that brought a smile. He peered down at the masses. They literally looked like a swarm of insects or rodents, scurrying in different directions.

'No wonder they call it the rat race,' he mumbled. It got quite bright on the platform as the sun shone through the huge panes of glass in the roof. Killian sat for a while until his coffee had drained; nothing appeared out of the ordinary. He was getting bored. Was anything actually going to happen today? He slumped back in his chair and didn't expect the middle-aged waitress when she approached. She leaned over and startled him when she reached out for his empty coffee cup. He could see up close her ample breasts in the tightly stretched black top she wore. He immediately sat up, pulled back in his seat, crumpling his newspaper.

'You finished with this, sir?' she asked sharply, already putting the cup on her tray before he'd even had a chance to answer.

'Oh, yeah, sorry,' he apologised, feeling a little awkward. He always was around women.

'You want anything else?' she quizzed, her face cast in stone.

Killian shook his head. He could tell that she was aggrieved as she walked away to the next table. She was scarier than a Gorgon he'd dealt with once. Killian was so preoccupied with the demon waitress that he nearly missed his target.

The wizard caught a glimpse of the boy and almost fell off his chair when he spotted him. There he was... Young Fagin! Killian pushed back his chair and stood. One or two people looked up from what they were doing when they heard the excruciating sound of the chair legs scraping the tiled floor. They gave a look of displeasure and returned to what they were doing. Killian realised that for someone who wanted to appear inconspicuous, he needed a bit more practice at tailing a suspect. But that was the last thing on his mind right now. He'd clocked his target and needed to keep him in his sights. The sunglasses were working perfectly. Not only did they reveal the spirit as a solid form, but they also picked up on the ectoplasm footprints he was leaving behind. It was more than he could have wished for.

'A trail of breadcrumbs,' he said, louder than he wanted, and a woman walking past gave him a strange glare. 'Er, for my new pet bird at home,' he said, looking back at her.

Killian's table was situated right next to the stairwell and that meant that he could follow his suspect without breaking eye contact. But he knew that that was the easy part. Finding spiritual beings was one thing; trapping one, was another problem entirely. Killian moved quickly down the steps, trying to dodge commuters. He huffed and puffed his way through and managed to get to the ground level without losing his suspect. Now he had to follow Young Fagin and keep himself concealed... and added to that, not look suspicious. He didn't need the station security hindering him and asking a load of embarrassing questions, while the thief got away.

Killian found a perfect spot where he could observe the boy. This was a train station, after all, and he knew that there were cameras all over the place. Killian took a breath. This was the closest he'd ever been to Fagin, to study him properly. Killian removed his sunglasses, slipped them in his pocket and trained his eyes on the young thief.

Young Fagin was a tall, slim lad, about fifteen or sixteen. His face was partially obscured by a woolly hat and the bum-fluff on his round chin. His eyes were jet black and his face pale and milky. Well, he was a ghost, after all. He was dressed in a tee-shirt with the title of a band splashed across the front. Killian didn't recognise the name, but he didn't know much about music anyway. The thief also wore faded, slightly baggy jeans and a pair of black trainers. He had a rucksack over his shoulder and that was where he stored his loot, Killian assumed. It was the perfect set up. He was invisible to his victims and really skilled at stealing items quickly.

He must have been doing this for years, Killian assumed, probably long before he'd died. And now in a supernatural state, he'd found a way of doing it all over again. He was very inventive and sophisticated because a poltergeist could normally only throw and move objects around. This guy had the ability to pick up and remove an object and carry it to store somewhere, ingenious. Killian was impressed. He'd never seen a supernatural being so organised. What the sorcerer couldn't work out was how Young Fagin was going to make money on his stolen items afterwards. He was living on a parallel plane. So how he was dealing with a fence to offload real objects was beyond Killian. This was a new level of ghost he was dealing with.

As he stood there observing, Killian pondered on the boy's backstory. How did he die so young? Why and how did he get involved in thieving? He appeared to be such an enterprising young lad. The world was robbed of this skilled, intelligent person before he had a chance to cut a life in the mortal world.

No one even realised that there was this ghost flitting through the station, gorging on unsuspecting victims' valuables. But Killian surmised that if someone really studied the video footage carefully, then at some point Fagin would be found out. So Killian waited and saw the boy sizing up his audience. He would strike soon and the wizard was poised ready to follow him back to his lair. And then Young Fagin sprang into action.

## Chapter 15
## Shadowed

Killian kept surveillance on his subject and didn't intervene. He wanted to follow the boy and find out where he kept his stash. Once he'd done that, he'd know where the ghost resided and hopefully confront him, then take steps to send him on to where he needed to continue his existence. Here was not the place this individual was supposed to be. He needed to go on to his final resting place and leave the mortal world to its devices.

Standing there watching, but hidden from view, Killian began to admire the skill this boy had. The ghost scrutinised each commuter and, like a panther stalking its prey, moved in and very nimbly, relieved them of their wallets, jewellery and anything else of value. The crowds began thinning out, either boarding or exiting the platform. Killian waited until he knew that the thief was ready to leave. But instead of disappearing, which would have made it difficult for Killian to track him, the boy walked off the platform just like the regular passengers. This was

Killian's chance to shadow him and see where he went. The warlock quickly put his sunglasses back on and followed the evidence through the visor. He kept as far back as he could.

Young Fagin sifted through the throng of people on the stairs, making his way out of the same gate that Killian had used to come into the station. The warlock observed that when the youngster drifted through solid bodies, the reactions on people's faces were mixed.

Some people wouldn't notice what was going on at all and carried on walking, which surprised Killian. Some though, one or two, stopped and shivered like they felt something real. It was the expression on their faces, a look of utter unpleasantness and fear. He saw one woman who was so shocked that she touched her chest, and her mouth fell wide open. She was tuned in to the dead on some level. She turned and glanced back, peering into the distance for a moment. Killian could see she was trying to puzzle something out. She took a deep breath and turned back and continued on her way.

Killian kept his distance, especially when the young crook walked out of the station. He'd kept surveillance for this long and didn't want to mess things up now. The boy strolled down the road and didn't appear to know that he was being followed. He was heading for a part of town that was unfamiliar to the wizard. Killian followed with interest and stealth. He knew a lot about spirits, ghosts and the like, being a sorcerer. He also understood that poltergeists didn't drift far from their resting place, so he wondered how far this entity had wandered from home. It couldn't have been that far or his power would weaken. The sun was beating down like a huge club, draining Killian's strength and drying out his mouth.

Young Fagin continued down towards the dock area of the town. He suddenly took a left turn and disappeared from view. Killian had to keep further back. There wasn't much cover and the teenager would have spotted him. Perhaps he already had.

'Shit,' Killian winced and broke into a jog. He didn't want to lose him now while he was so close. When he got to the turning and he tentatively poked his head around the edge of the wall. 'Fuck,' he groaned. It was a dead end. He scratched his head nervously because he could feel there was something there. He stepped out into the open. This didn't feel good.

He looked around and saw that there were several large warehouse doors to his left. The huge wooden panels were on sliders, like an aircraft hangar. To his right was a brick wall. At the back end of the wide expanse was another wall, which connected the two sides like a cul-de-sac. Killian slowly walked along the centre of the lane. He kept his eyes peeled for any movement. There was no way out above because the buildings and the walls were high and towered over him. He scanned the floor for any signs of ectoplasm and felt relief when he saw something glistening on the ground.

'He definitely stood here,' Killian whispered and as he stooped down, to take a closer look, he muttered, 'Yep, that's his DNA all right.'

A voice spoke from behind him and cut through his thoughts. Killian froze and grimaced — he'd been found out.

'You looking for me?' The voice was filled with anger and Killian was reluctant to turn. But he knew he had to and slowly spun around to face him. He knew immediately that he was boxed in. The poltergeist stood between him and his exit. And Killian also knew that these spirits were very powerful.

'Hi, kid,' Killian answered meekly.

'Well, here I am,' the boy said and the ghostly figure walked towards the wizard. 'Why are you following me, wizard? What do you want with me?' he said, his face twisted with hate.

'Me? Looking for you? Nah. I don't even know you, kid,' Killian said shaking his head. 'Wizard? What are you talking about?' Killian mocked but could see it wasn't working. The situation was already escalating.

'Don't fucking call me kid, wizard,' the boy scowled, baring his teeth. 'Why are you following me?' he questioned angrily.

'Okay, okay. Let's not be hasty,' Killian stalled. 'Give me a chance to explain.'

But the boy wasn't in the mood for negotiating. He'd already made up his mind. 'I don't like you,' he spat and with that raised his hands, sending a shockwave of white energy from the tips of his fingers. Killian didn't have time to react. The rippling and sparking coils wrapped around his body like electrically charged ropes. He'd never felt pain like it in his entire life. It took his breath away. He couldn't move and fell to the ground, his sunglasses slipping off his face. The youngster — still sending the blasts of energy — stepped on the frames and crushed them into the cobbles.

'Aaaaaargh, shut it off, please. Shut it off,' Killian pleaded and was wriggling around the ground in agony. The boy intensified the level of power, which made Killian scream out. '*For fuck's sake, stop it, please!*' The warlock begged liked he'd never done before. He felt as though a million electrified needles were attacking his whole body. His eyeballs were on fire and his heart felt like it was about to burst. He was shaking uncontrollably. '*Please stop!*' he said, grovelling on the ground, teeth clenched together. The world was spinning around him at a million miles per hour and he felt as if he was about to throw up over the stones.

The young thief leaned in, a smile curling his mouth. 'Why are you fucking following me?' he raged. 'I don't know you, so why are you after me, fucking dick? If you're not a wizard, then how can you see me? Oh, by the way,' he smirked and added, 'you're also really crap at shadowing people. That won't matter before long, though.'

Killian was shaking violently and found it difficult to speak. It was like the worst flu he'd ever encountered — he felt hot and cold all at the same time. He pushed the boundaries tried to speak. 'I'm n-ot foll-owing you.' He tried to get the words out but didn't have full control of his mouth. His tongue was numb and his teeth ached. But what he did realise, there and then, was that this kid wasn't going to let go until he'd killed him, that was for sure. This was a one-way ticket and Killian could see the hatred in the young man's eyes. This was no fun-loving teenager. He was angry at something or someone and was taking it all out on him.

Young Fagin was a killer, pure and simple, and Killian was next on his list. He had to think of something right now, or it was all over. Even though his mind was buzzing, Killian dug deep. The boy still had his arms outstretched and fingers flayed as he walked around his victim, pounding the wizard with his poltergeist energy.

He was still laughing, enjoying the pure torture he was inflicting. He was enjoying it a little too much. The wizard could have done with someone walking past, to break this boy's concentration. But that never happened when you needed a police officer or a witness to come along. He was on his own and so close to death.

Killian managed to dip his hand into his pocket and grasp his wand without Young Fagin seeing what he was doing. It was difficult, but he focused his mind and pushed the pain away, just for a second or two. Luckily for him, the boy by now was laughing so manically that he closed his eyes. And that was the wizard's only chance, and he quickly pulled out his wand. He whispered a spell and the wand instantly crackled into life. He hoped it would work. Killian managed to send an invisible blast of energy from the wand, right at Fagin's chest. The boy saw it coming but he could do nothing to stop it. The magical spell hit him off his feet and propelled his ghostly body through the air. He slammed into the wall and disappeared through to the other side.

That was all that Killian needed. The electrical charge was instantly broken off and the pain ceased in a split second. He gulped for air. Killian's body relaxed from the spasm, but he didn't have time to rest. He felt relief and coldness all at the same time, as if going cold turkey. The attack had left him with a huge drain in energy. But he knew that he had to be ready for another attack straight away. Young Fagin would soon want his revenge and Killian had to be ready to retaliate.

So, even though he was exhausted, he got rather shakily to his feet. He thought he was going to pass out and throw up at the same time. Every fibre in his body ached. He was trembling and coughing and trying to swallow. His head was as light as the wind. He breathed hard and felt like crying.

'Pull yourself together, Spooks,' he grunted. Killian shuffled to his left and fell against the wall for support. 'That hurt too,' he moaned. It was all he could do to stay conscious. But he was breathing easier now and his focus was coming back.

'Jesus, that kid is strong,' he mumbled to himself. 'One more blast like that and I'm toast,' he gasped. He held out his wand, and his arm was trembling; sweat poured down his face. He felt so weak, a stiff wind would have blown him over. He tried to reassert himself. 'Snap out of it, Killian, you've dealt with worse than this. Where is that fucking thug?' Killian quickly flicked his eyes from left to right. The problem he had was that he didn't know in what direction the teenager would attack.

He waited and waited, arm extended, eyes slightly blurred and legs like jelly. He was breathing in laboured gasps and his tongue felt dry and tingly. He couldn't gather spit inside his mouth. What he wouldn't do for a glass of water. The heat of the day was taxing enough. On the other hand, the feeling was coming back to his limbs and his body still prickled, but his strength was returning. The difference this time was that he would be ready and could fight back. His wizard's intuition told him that something was about to appear behind, so he spun around and almost fell over as he did so. With his head still foggy and his eyes slightly out of focus, Killian could see his enemy, a split second before the thief could completely materialise, and that was all he needed. He urgently mumbled another spell.

# Chapter 16
# Trapped

The thief appeared but was immediately caught inside a magical and unbreakable bubble, like a giant snow globe. When Young Fagin realised what was going on, he went berserk. From inside he began screaming, kicking and punching in a bid to break through. When he knew it wasn't happening, he made offensive gestures towards the wizard. All Killian got was all the rude signage, and pent-up anger, but everything was muted.

Killian peered back at the youngster and noticed how vulnerable this kid now appeared. Once he'd settled down then he could see how scared the boy looked. Killian felt sorry for the young lad, but he couldn't let him out right away. There was much too much anger inside him. Killian needed to figure out how to release him from the bubble and send him directly to his true destination. Why was he filled with so much hatred? And the wizard had felt the brunt of it all.

Killian took a breath. He was still aching, but the weakness he'd endured from the fight was wearing off; his strength was returning. He could stand up with confidence. He studied the young thief and saw something had suddenly changed about his persona. Killian also thought he felt another presence close by and that unnerved him. The wizard was confused and he didn't enjoy this uneasy feeling. There was something about to happen, he could sense it.

Young Fagin's eyes widened and terror filled every nook and cranny of his face. Killian realised that the boy wasn't in charge any more. And soon after… the pain that the young thug had inflicted - started all over again. Killian was right there, caught in its grip. He was in agony and his head thumped as if a sledgehammer was pummelling his mind. But he noticed in all the confusion that the magic wasn't coming from the boy this time. How could it? He was trapped inside Killian's entrapment spell. The power was emerging from some other outside, source. Killian quickly dipped his hand into his pocket. The pain soon got so immense that he had to let go of the wand. He cupped his head with his hands to try and ease the gigantic headache emerging inside his skull.

'Jesus Christ, what the fuck is going on?' he shrieked. 'Not again.' He fell to his knees, the pressure like a vice, squeezing the life force out of him. Young Fagin was immediately released from the spell and stood trembling, eyes glassy and filled with sheer, panic. Killian couldn't turn around to see who was behind. The power that rained down on him was so immense, even worse than when Young Fagin was doing it. Then he heard its voice.

'This pathetic excuse for a fucking wizard beat you, you little shit,' the voice scolded in a booming tirade.

Killian wanted to intervene but couldn't; everything was out of his control. This was the reason for everything bad about the boy. Killian was sure of it. He was being bullied, pure and simple. The mortal world had bullies and so too did the immortal world, and Killian hated bullies.

'I-I...' Young Fagin tried to answer but was stopped. The boy, though he too was a spirit, was physically shaking as a human would. He was terrified of this force.

'Shut the fuck up,' the voice immediately closed him off. 'Now grab his wand and let's dispose of this prick,' he demanded. The voice was evil and grated the mind, like cutting through tin with a hacksaw. Killian managed to turn around even though a thousand electric shocks were roasting his body. He saw a tall man standing there. His features were old and grizzled. The shadow from his wide-brimmed hat cast deep gouges in his face. He wore a long coat on his slim frame. And, Killian sensed that... he wasn't a ghost. He was a supernatural of some kind and definitely wielding magic from his hands. In fact, he felt closer to it being a wizard, but not quite.

'What is it with these hot needles? Killian raged, only just about managing to get his words out. 'Who the fuck are you?'

'None of your business, lowlife,' he jeered, exposing brown teeth that hadn't seen a toothbrush in a hundred years. 'You're going to die today though, that's a fact,' he said with a smile and then turned on the boy once again. 'Pick up his fucking wand if you know what's good for you, kid,' the man raged.

While he was distracted, Killian dug deep inside himself again and aimed his last ounce of energy at a shard of slate, which lay on the ground next to him. It took everything he had to firstly make it tremble. The guy couldn't see what was happening because Killian's body was hunched over, obscuring the view.

The slither of slate suddenly whipped up from the ground, moving like a missile. It embedded itself just above the eye of the creature, making him scream. The dagger dug deep into his temple and for a moment he lost concentration. Killian collapsed to the ground as most of the pressure was lifted. But the wizard's magic was almost used up. The creature was disorientated as the blood oozed from the fresh wound and leaked into his eye, blinding his left side. As he tried to wipe away the stream with his hand, he also compromised his right eye. So now he was partially blinded on both sides. He still held Killian in his power, though.

'Fucking, wizard,' he yelled and tried to intensify the energy he was already inflicting. But as soon as he did so... it stopped — he stopped! Killian's body relaxed again but the warlock didn't have the strength to push himself up.

Young Fagin couldn't believe what was happening. He saw the man blasted right off his feet as if hit by a cannonball. His body flew across the ground and crashed into the wall on the other side. He was down.

Killian found a small pocket of strength and managed to push himself onto his back. When he looked up, he saw into the beautiful, blue eyes of Cleo Smoke. She was standing a little further back and could see the pain he was in. She looked back at him and that was her mistake. There was another flash of white lightning, which propelled her completely off her feet. She tumbled along the gravel, her black hair flailing in the wind, body contorted.

Killian managed to push himself up into a sitting position. It was so difficult — every muscle seemed to scream out. He could see his wand. Young Fagin hadn't had time to pick it up. Killian forgot about the pain and rushed to grab it. He was now running on adrenaline and turned on his attacker... but the creature had already disappeared.

'Shit, shit, shit!' Killian ranted. 'Where'd he go? Where the hell is he?' Killian immediately turned towards Young Fagin and discovered that he'd disappeared too. He looked over to Cleo, who was getting back on her feet, still looking a bit unsteady.

'Who the fuck was that?' she winced, dusting herself down.

'Like I would know,' Killian answered, 'never seen him before.' Now the wizard had two problems: Young Fagin, who he now realised was doing all this because he was forced into it; the second problem was this new being. Why couldn't life be easy? he pondered. 'Thanks for coming to help, Cleo,' he said gratefully. 'You really saved my bacon.'

'No problem, glad you called me,' she replied.

'I literally had a split second to send a signal with my phone and I'm glad you picked up on it,' he said.

She walked over to him and offered her hand so that he could get back to his feet. 'You really don't know who he is?' she probed. 'He's strong. I've never fought someone as powerful as that before,' Cleo admitted.

'I've no idea who or what he is, Cleo,' Killian said and shook his head.

'And who is the boy?' She had more questions than he could answer.

He looked at her and smiled. 'The boy is my case — the guy is what's causing the boy to do what he's doing, which is stealing from over there.' Killian pointed in the direction of the train station. 'But it looks like I have to solve one part, to sort out the other. I have to find that kid and get him away from that force. Once I have him safe, then I have to work out how to trap that... well, whatever it is. The boy is really scared. I hope that thing doesn't have him trapped, but it doesn't look good from what I can see.' He looked bitter when he said it. 'The boy needs to go onto his next place. And that creature needs to be destroyed. He's using him for his own needs. And the boy is too scared to fight back against it.'

Killian walked over to where the guy had landed. He knelt down... with a great groan. Everything was sensitive. To be fair, he knew his body had taken a beating in the last few days. He definitely needed some R and R. Killian tried to put the pain to the back of his mind and studied the ground, looking for some clue to his DNA. It was hard to concentrate.

'What are you looking for?' Cleo asked as she followed him.

'Ah. This,' he said and dipped into his pocket for a small glass vial. She watched as he unscrewed the metal top. He then scooped up a small amount of black residue with a paddle he kept inside the tube. He quickly screwed the top back on.

'What is that?' she said and seemed really interested. 'Are you Sherlock Holmes now?' They looked at each other and chuckled.

'Kind of, my dear Cleo,' he answered with a grin, 'but without the floppy hat and corduroy trousers.' She laughed. 'This will hopefully lead to him, but first I have to find that kid. He can't be far from here. I just hope that he's safe. Poltergeists can't wander too distantly from their homing ground,' he said. 'And that has to be nearby. He must be somewhere inside the train yard.'

'Do you need help with that?' Cleo asked. She looked as though she didn't want to go back to where ever she'd just come from. Killian smiled.

'I called you, didn't I? Come on. I think I know where he is,' Killian said with confidence. They walked back out onto the road. 'That kid manoeuvred me like a chess piece in that cul-de-sac.' He showed Cleo where they'd just come from. 'I was stupid enough to fall for his trick and that was my first mistake.'

'Wow. The great Killian Spooks admitting that he's made a mistake,' she mused.

'Shut up,' he said. 'I also underestimated how intelligent and powerful that kid is too,' Killian admitted, rolling his head from side to side. 'I think he was actually heading for the old train yard around the back of this place when I was following him. That place is where old train carriages are kept if they've gone into disrepair. They'd eventually get decommissioned. It's a goldmine for train nuts, but no one else would bother even going there. I think it's the perfect place to hold up. And I also think that he's got a train car in there somewhere.'

'You think he's here?' Cleo said sceptically. The yard was a big area. There were lots of variations of train cars there. It was going to be a formidable task to find the one that Young Fagin was hiding in.

'It's where I would go if life treated me badly,' he said honestly.

'Where do we start?' Cleo asked as she gazed at the array of old wagons.

'That's where I have to concentrate.' Killian stood for a moment and dropped the vial with the residue in his pocket. He had to find this kid with just wizard's intuition. He closed his eyes and smiled. He looked up and pointed. 'There!'

There was a carriage which was singled out from the others. Killian nodded to Cleo and they steadily walked towards it.

# Chapter 17
## Uninvited guests

Cleo and Killian carefully approached the railway car. It was the only one remotely parked from the others in the yard. The carriage had been sitting there for several years by the look of it. The wheels were welded into position with mud, grass and a wooden chock on both sides. It appeared much older and classier than the rest of the collection. Killian assumed it was because it was an antique or classic and that's why they'd kept it apart.

He didn't know anything about trains, but this one was made of wood and even he knew that those types of carriages were long gone. The car was shorter than the others too and its timber frame was rotten. It was reddish, although faded now, and in its day, it must have been brightly painted, like a post-box. If Killian needed to hide, he'd have chosen this one too. His wizard's sense told him that there was certainly a supernatural presence inside. He stood firm for a moment, just to take in the spiritual waves that emitted from there. The heat in the railway yard was sweltering and Killian knew it was going to be hot as hell in there too.

'You, all right?' Cleo asked, a little concerned.

'I'm fine, it's definitely this one, Cleo,' he said, 'I can feel it.'

'Okay,' she nodded, but wasn't getting anything spiritually from it at all. 'How do we do this?' she added. 'This is a dry goods car,' she said and Killian looked at her incredulously. 'What?' she said returning the look.

'A dry goods car?' Killian grinned. 'How do you know that, Miss Smoke? Are you a train spotter?' he mocked. 'Do you spend your spare time jotting down engine numbers?'

'No,' she said, and appeared miffed, 'shut it, Killian.'

'If you like trains that's fine,' Killian said, 'I'm not judging.'

'Can we move on now, please?' She sounded annoyed and when she was, he noticed that she twisted her nose, which crinkled at the bridge. She was cute. He shook the thought from his mind. Number one… Cleo was a lesbian. And number two, he had a lovely girlfriend anyway. Life was complicated enough.

'Yep, fine,' Killian agreed and turned serious. 'Can you keep a lookout for that guy while I go inside?' She looked at him as if to ask why she couldn't go in with him. 'Forgive the pun,' he added, 'but two of us will spook him, even though he's technically a spook himself,' Killian joked. 'I saw how scared he was of that thug and it's going to be difficult enough, alone,'

'I get it,' she said agreeing with him. 'Do you think he'll come back?' she said, meaning the nasty piece of work they'd only just encountered.

'We've got to be prepared. He's bound to come back at some point. He wants the boy and we're in his way,' he said and turned towards the sliding doors. He looked at the dividers. The rest of the carriage was falling apart, but these were amazingly still pretty much intact. There was a gap in the middle where the doors were slightly parted. Someone at some point had gone inside for the night. Perhaps they were still in there. Killian had to expect anything and be on his guard.

He tentatively popped his head inside the unit, sweeping his gaze from one end to the other. It was pretty dark in there apart from a few of holes in the roof, which let in spots of sunlight. There was nothing in there apart from some old sacking strewn about on the floor, and hanging from the ceiling a couple of metal hooks. Whoever kept security in this place wouldn't even bat an eyelid. It wasn't even watertight so travellers would probably choose a dryer car to sleep in.

Killian then spotted some more sacks, further to the other end. These were piled up with a bulge in the centre. The wizard assumed that perhaps that's where all the loot from the thefts was kept. The kid had to be down that end.

He climbed onto the rusted metal footrest and stepped inside. He instantly felt the coldness of the room, which gave him the first clue that something was there. Outside it was a hot summer's day and Killian flicked his gaze over his shoulder and could see the heat haze lifting from the track. But inside the car was as cold as midwinter. He breathed a mouthful of steaming mist, which clouded the air in front of his eyes and quickly evaporated. He shivered as the chilled air entered his lungs. The heat from outside was calling to him, but he had to sort this out. The sorcerer walked quietly to the centre of the carriage and stood with his eyes closed. This was the best way in which he could pinpoint his target accurately. The cold air weighed heavy on his chest, which made breathing more difficult. Killian concentrated his mind, reaching for his deeper senses.

'I know you're here,' he said, his voice cutting through the sound of creaking timbers. 'I'm here to help you. I'm not here to harm you.' Killian said, still not opening his eyes. 'You know that I'm not the enemy here, right? I was the victim out there, wasn't I? Whatever that is, we can deal with it together and get you to where you need to go.' There was nothing in return, only silence, but Killian knew he was listening. 'I am only here to help you.' Killian spoke again. He felt a sense of anger and opened his eyes. It was just in time too. He quickly had to step to one side when an iron hook whizzed past his head and embedded itself in the wooden panel behind him. Killian breathed hard. 'Take it easy, ki...' he was about to say kid but thought better of it. He didn't want to antagonise this boy any more than he needed to. 'Take it easy,' Killian repeated. Then the silence was broken.

'Stay the fuck away from me, wizard. I don't need you or anyone else.' Young Fagin's voice ripped from the shadows and washed over Killian like an icy shower. 'Why did you come here? You've only made things worse. He'll work me twice as hard now and beat me twice as bad,' the boy cried in anger. The air sizzled with electricity.

'Please calm down.' And Killian immediately winced. No one ever responded positively to that instruction. 'Look. My name is Killian Spooks,' Killian quickly responded.

'Are you shitting me?' The boy mocked. Killian hated this part. The number of times that he had to explain himself — it always came out the same. Spooks wasn't a good name for a wizard to have, if you didn't want to be made fun of, that is. But what could he do? It was his name.

'Yes, kid, it really is,' Killian continued. 'Who I am is not important. The most important thing here is getting you home.' Killian shook his head; this was not going at all well.

'I'm not a kid,' Fagin rasped and Killian realised he'd already messed up.

'Yeah, okay. I apologise,' Killian said and added in a lighter tone, 'What's your name? I can't talk to someone without knowing who I'm talking to.' Killian was trying to re-establish a friendly line of communication with the boy. There was a pause and he had a sense that the boy spirit was warming to him.

'Brad,' he said after a few moments silence — the anger was subsiding. The wizard peered into the darkened end of the trailer. Something was happening. He could see a figure forming. Firstly, there was a slight disturbance in the dust molecules that were freely floating around. Then, there he was, standing, a luminous figure hovering in the corner of the carriage. He looked as innocent and harmless as he'd done when he was trapped in the bubble. This was just a kid who was vulnerable and alone. He certainly didn't deserve the treatment that was being inflicted on him by that overbearing entity.

'Hi, Brad, it's nice to meet you,' Killian said warmly. 'Why don't you come a little closer? I promise you that I won't harm you.'

He did tentatively hover along in his suspended form towards the warlock. 'What do you want with me, wizard? Do you want to use me too?' Brad asked, still not using Killian's name.

'Killian, please. No, definitely not. I want to help you, Brad,' Killian said honestly. 'I don't want anything from you, I promise. You're in a bad situation, which is not being helped by that bully.' Even saying the word made Killian shudder.

'What? You want to help me like Killjoy wanted to help me?' Brad hissed. 'Use me like a puppet?' He could already feel the anger starting to build again.

'Is that his name?' Killian pressed. 'Sounds about right. He has been a bit of a kill joy already.'

This made the boy, let slip a smile and Killian returned the gesture. 'Yeah. Drake Killjoy.' The boy spoke his name with real distaste and the warmth vanished. 'He's a nasty shit. All he wants are the goods and he'll do anything to get them. I suppose you want my stuff too?' The hatred was coming through thick and fast.

'No, Brad, I don't want your stuff,' Killian said, shaking his head. 'All I want to do is send you on to where you're supposed to be. You belong somewhere that's safe and where you can spend the rest of your existence in peace. I want to get you away from people like Drake Killjoy, believe me?'

Brad was starting to believe Killian. He was slowly getting through. 'He'll find me. He always does,' Brad said solemnly. 'I've moved from place to place and he always finds me,' Brad continued, tears in his eyes. 'I can't escape him.'

'I can change that. He won't find you… he can't go where you are going,' Killian said with conviction, his eyes wide and bitterness filtering into his tone. 'He doesn't want you to go where you're supposed to go. Because once you're there, he won't be able to reach you any more. It's the one place where he's not invited. I promise you,' Killian assured him. The boy was softening — responding to his offer.

And, with that Killian heard Cleo's scream from outside.

'He's here,' Brad hardened again. 'You've brought him here. He'll kill you and your friend.'

'No! He's not getting you this time, Brad,' Killian insisted. 'I'm a wizard and stronger than he is. Stay here, please. I will sort this out once and for

176

all,' Killian pleaded. Brad looked deep into Killian's green eyes and nodded. 'Please, whatever happens, stay put.'

Killian climbed down from the dry goods car with wand in hand, the tip already crackling with magical energy. He immediately saw Cleo on the ground, eyes closed, not moving. Killian's stomach tightened. He knelt and hovered his palm over her chest — she was only unconscious — he breathed a sigh. He looked around. Everything was quiet. The sun was high and the sky a crystal blue. He could feel the warm air and it was a welcome feeling from the cold inside the goods carriage. He stood up when he saw a figure standing on the gravel, only a matter of twenty metres away. Killian stood facing his enemy. It was like something from an old spaghetti western. But there must only be one winner here and Killian hoped it was going to be him. He spread out his shoulders and appeared taller. He didn't break eye contact from Drake Killjoy. The old guy smirked.

'So, prick. You think you can beat me?' Drake Killjoy chuckled. 'Time to die.'

'No, dickhead, I know I can beat you,' Killian grinned. 'There's only one going to die here today, so give up now.'

'Prepare for pain, little wizard…'

# Chapter 18
## Wizard versus Who?

They stood for a few, quiet moments staring each other down, both trying to get the better of the other.

'So, what are you, Drake Killjoy?' Killian questioned. 'I can feel your energy, but can't quite pinpoint your origin. You're a nasty piece of work, I know that.'

'Oh, so the little shit told you who I am?' Killjoy responded with a sneer. 'I'll fix him later after I've dealt with you.'

'Yep. And what you've been making him do,' Killian continued through gritted teeth. 'That's called bullying where I come from, pure and simple.'

'Well, someone has to do it—' Killjoy was about to finish.

'Not really,' Killian cut in smartly. 'Pricks just take advantage of the weak.'

'And why not do it to a poltergeist?' He grinned broadly showing those awful teeth again. 'They're scum, aren't they?'

'Please, close your mouth. You're giving rats a bad name with that stinking breath,' Killian said and could see his grin disappear. 'Again, what are you?' Killian pressed.

'You're a cheeky fucking punk,' Killjoy growled. 'Before I tell you anything, who are you?' Killjoy rounded. 'I need to know who I'm going to kill today,' he said pleasantly.

Killian blurted out a chuckle. This guy was confident. 'Killian Spooks is the name,' Killian said proudly, waiting for the obvious taunts about his surname.

'Nope. Never heard of you,' Killjoy responded. 'As I thought — a nobody, ah well, who cares anyway?' He stood rigid. There was a slight wind that whipped up dust around his feet and rippled the tails of his long black coat. He did appear a formidable sight, like a baddie from an old western. 'Let's get on with this. I've other fish to fry.' The confidence in this spirit was annoying, to say the least.

'Yes, the bullying of helpless spirits won't do itself, will it? I'm all for getting rid of the likes of you,' Killian shot back. 'So, before we start. What are you? You still haven't told me. I like to know who I'm dealing with.' This time he was demanding to know. 'You're not a wizard, thank God. You're not a fairy. Or a troll — could be a boggart or a necromancer,' Killian joked and hoped he wasn't the latter.

'A fairy?' Drake Killjoy laughed out loud. 'No. Not a fairy. I'm a shaman of the highest order. I'm *the* shaman.' Killjoy nodded and touched the edge of his wide-brimmed hat with theatrical flair.

'I don't know about shaman. But you are a shame to your kind, I know that,' Killian spat. With that Killjoy's face changed and he peered back at Killian with his black eyes. 'Is all this to do with greed? You get the kid to do your dirty work and reap the benefits?' Killian dug in.

'Yes. It's all about the money,' he said shamelessly. 'Come on… it's fool proof. I get a poltergeist to get the loot and there are no witnesses. No one is ever going to find me, are they? And all he has to do is disappear. Win-win.' He was right of course; it was a fool proof idea. But it was also a continuing cycle and a lot of misery for the boy. 'Enough of this banter,' Killjoy snarled, 'this conversation is over. Now shut the fuck up and let me save you the trouble of living,' he said and didn't waste any more time.

He raised his hands and levitated a loose railway sleeper from the ground and sent it flying towards Killian's head. The wizard immediately rolled out of the way as it smashed straight through an old signal box — obliterating it into tiny splinters. He laughed out loud at the prank. As he stood smugly, Killian uttered a spell that slammed into the shaman. It sent him tumbling, thirty metres along the gravel path between train carriages. He stopped in a tangle of arms and legs. When he finally got to his feet he was fuming and shouted to Killian with a load of obscenities.

'You fucking bastard,' he bellowed and let rip with a mini tornado. Killian was running hard in his pursuit, but the swirling wind caught his feet. It spun him around and lifted him ten metres into the air. While he was trying to push against the magic, Killjoy flicked his fingers. Killian went spiralling across the sky and landed, with a thud on the gravel between two cars.

'Oh, that mongrel,' he hissed. The wizard recovered quickly and clambered back out into the open. For a split-second he couldn't see Killjoy, but he held his wand in readiness. Then, he stepped out from a small, wooden hut and stood in the section where he'd originally landed — the space between two carriages.

Killjoy immediately blasted electrical charges of devastating power from his fingers, which were aimed directly at Killian's midsection. But Killian was wise to it and held out his wand. The stream of magic that emitted from the tip had created a large defensive shield, which immediately blocked and deflected the attack. Killjoy's powerful tendrils danced and struck the armour that protected Killian's body, but couldn't penetrate the sphere.

Killjoy intensified his attack and added wild blue fire to melt Killian's magical dome. The flames lashed at the orb in an inferno of fire and smoke. It was an intense force, but Killian stood calmly inside and concentrated his mind, trying to keep safe from the wild storm outside. It was getting more and more difficult to keep his magic at a steady pace.

Shit, this Shaman is pretty strong, Killian was thinking as he pushed back with all his might. He couldn't let this menace take over, but Killian could feel the power of the entity heighten as he bombarded his defences. He could also hear the wild laughter and realised how much the shaman was enjoying the fight. It was no wonder he'd made so many lives a misery. The confidence he had was incredible. This made the wizard even angrier. He thought of the boy in the train car. He thought of Cleo on the ground. If Drake Killjoy defeated him today, then Cleo would be destroyed and Brad would be under his control forever.

Killjoy let loose with everything he had, but couldn't see exactly what was happening. No one had ever survived this surge and the shaman was confident that he'd killed off the wizard. The brilliant magic created a blinding screen on the surface of the bubble and Drake Killjoy screamed out in wild laughter as he bombarded the wizard with more, pure energy. The snaking tendrils twisted and slapped against the surface and the fire continued to burn bright blue.

Killian's eyes were closed and he could feel the heat building up inside the bubble. His breathing was urgent and his powers waning. He didn't know how much longer he could keep going, but he was also, slowly, draining Killjoy's power too, he assumed. Killian could feel the nerves in his stomach tightened — his face was creased up into a tight ball. Sweat was drenching his body. What if this shaman was stronger than him? Fuck it, he thought. I'm not going to give in.

'Die you bastard — die,' Drake Killjoy screamed and continued to blast the deadly ray from his fingers. Killian's clothes were sodden, and his body felt like a ton weight. His vision became blurred as dizziness prevailed. He felt as if he was going to throw up and swallowed back hard. His breathing became erratic and surely the end now was in sight? It was at that point, that things suddenly began to change. Killian sensed the shaman's power weakening. He flicked his eyes open with a renewed belief that he could defeat this guy. This invigorated him to dig as deep as he'd ever done before. Killian lent his mind to the elders and dug into a reserve magical stream.

He sent his last surge of magic and hoped for the best. The reverse polarity exploded the bubble and traced the lines of energy, right back to the source. The power was too much for the shaman to handle. The bubble disintegrated and now Killian was exposed, but Drake Killjoy's power was broken and the fire and tendrils died.

Killjoy screamed as the extra magical energy blasted him through the air, like a large missile. He smashed through two train carriages in an explosion of debris. The air was filled with splintered glass, wood and metal. A great cloud of dust mushroomed towards the sky as if a nuclear blast had erupted and then… everything calmed.

Killian fell to his knees, still grasping the wand. He'd been pummelled and was at his weakest point. He knew he couldn't stay where he was. He had to find Killjoy. He had to finally finish him off. So, with great difficulty, he pushed himself upright and unsteadily stood on his feet. The heat was blistering from the cloudless, blue expanse. He felt sick and feeble. He could barely put one foot in front of the other. But there was still

a job to do and if Killjoy regained his strength —
then nothing would stop him.

Killian looked ahead and saw the tangled
mess where the two carriages once stood. But there
was no sign of Drake Killjoy. Where the fuck was
he? He held his wand, ready for another
encounter. Maybe, he had destroyed him? Killian
shook his head at that thought. This wasn't going
to be that easy.

The warlock stumbled along the ground,
barely holding himself upright. He could hear the
sound of someone groaning from behind but
didn't look back. He assumed it was Cleo coming
to. At least he hoped it was. He also wanted to
check in on Brad, but this was not the time. He
needed to find Drake Killjoy right away and end
this. He couldn't let him get away again. When he
finally approached the ruined train cars, he looked
straight through the hole the shaman's body had
created. Apart from jagged metal and a million
splinters of glass fragments, there was nothing.

'*Fuck*. Where are you, Killjoy?' Killian shouted.
His voice boomed across the yard. '*Killjoy!*' he
bellowed, and stood panting. He walked around
the carriages but kept his wits about him. There
was nothing there of the shaman, but on the
ground, he did see a small piece of material. Killian
picked it up and examined it closely. It was black

and looked like the same cloth from the coat that Killjoy was wearing, only moments earlier. It had fresh blood on it, but no sign of its owner. He was gone and Killian closed his eyes in frustration. He'd let him get away. Killian shrugged off all the pain and focused.

'*Killjoy!*' he screamed and his voice was whipped away by the wind.

Killian put his wand in his pocket — he didn't need it now. He interlocked his fingers at the back of his skull and stretched his back. His face was a picture of annoyance at himself. He should have finished this there and then. He puffed out a mouthful of air and turned back towards Cleo, who was slumped on the ground next to Brad's hiding place. She was rubbing her head and looked sheepishly at Killian. When he got closer to her, her demeanour told him everything. He staggered over and helped her to her feet.

'Are you okay?' he asked.

'I'm sorry, Killian,' she responded.

Killian shook his head and looked her in the eyes. 'Not your fault, Cleo,' he said.

'I should have been ready,' she grimaced. 'It was my job to protect the kid and he caught me off guard. I'm so stupid.'

'Stop beating yourself up, Cleo. He's a powerful and crafty piece of work. It took all I had to keep him at bay. On the bright side though, if there is one, I think he's gone from this world for now,' Killian assumed. 'I don't think though it's the last time I'll be crossing paths with Mr Drake Killjoy.' Even saying his name made Killian angry. 'I have to let it go and help who I can right now, and that is Brad.'

In a million years will be too soon for me to meet this guy again,' Cleo confessed.

'So you know his name now?' she asked. 'He's opened up to you then?'

Killian leaned against the tram and closed his eyes. He ran his tongue along the underside of his front teeth. 'Yeah. I kind of found a way to connect with him,' Killian said, rolling his shoulders and gritting his teeth. He continued. 'He won't be happy that Killjoy is still at large though. But that won't matter if I can send him on his way.'

'And I thought Relic was bad enough, but this other character is even worse,' Cleo sighed.

'Thank you, Cleo. Thanks for coming to help me when I needed you. If it hadn't been for your distraction then I think things would have turned out a lot different,' Killian admitted.

'Glad to have been of help,' she said, 'but I wish I could have put up more of a fight.'

'You were dealing with a shaman,' Killian added and that made Cleo Smoke stare right back into his eyes. 'What is it?' Killian pressed.

'My father was killed by a shaman.' This made Cleo stop and think. 'It's a long shot, but do you think it could be the same one? I never knew his name.'

'Maybe you'll have a chance to ask him one day,' Killian responded.

'Maybe,' she nodded.

'Hey, Brad. Come out here. It's time for you to go home, my friend,' Killian said, but he didn't appear and Killian realised that he must still be scared.

# Chapter 19
## The Journey Home

Killian and Cleo climbed into the dry goods truck when the boy didn't emerge. They found him standing there in his pale, luminous form. He looked scared — eyes filled with anguish. This was the boy that Killian knew was inside that brash, young arrogant teen. The wizard knew he had to be tough just to keep undesirables away. But when Drake Killjoy found Brad, then he took full advantage and used him for his evil plans. The warlock couldn't imagine how lonely and scared this individual must have felt before Killjoy got his claws into him. Then how tough he had to be to steal and deliver the stolen goods to the evil shaman.

'Where is he?' Brad trembled. He was almost crying. 'He's going to get me. You should have wiped him off the face of the earth. Now he'll come back for me.'

'He won't bother you any more, Brad, that's for sure,' Killian assured him, 'he's gone. Where you are going, he won't ever be able to hurt you again.'

The boy couldn't believe it and stayed silent for a moment. He then looked at Cleo with glassy, sad eyes. 'Who is she, Killian?' he asked, sceptical of everyone. 'Was it her voice we heard from outside?'

'Yeah, that's right. This is Cleo Smoke. She's my very good friend,' Killian said and she smiled. 'Without her, things would have been a lot different today. You should thank her. She took on a force she wasn't expecting.'

'Thank you, Cleo Smoke,' the boy said gratefully and stared at her. He was a teenager and she was gorgeous. Being a poltergeist didn't change the fact that he was a young man. And seeing a girl as pretty as Cleo didn't mean he couldn't be attracted to her.

'You can close your mouth now, Brad. You're barking up the wrong tree, mate,' Killian said and could see that Brad was confused.

'Killian,' Cleo said and punched him in the shoulder.

'Ouch, that hurt,' he complained.

'You're embarrassing the boy,' she said. 'I'm gay, Brad,' Cleo said, rolling her eyes.

'Oh wow. I get it now, no need to explain,' he responded.

'Are you two... you know... together?' Brad asked. 'Because you can totally have a boyfriend and girlfriend even though you're—' He was about to carry on when Killian stopped him dead.

'Nooooo. Not at all,' both Cleo and Killian answered at the same time.

'I know all about the bisexual thing, Brad, but no. Can we please change the conversation?' Cleo insisted and for the first time since Killian had known her, she looked embarrassed. He chuckled when he saw her cheeks turn from a white porcelain to beetroot red.

'Wow, okay,' Brad was grinning and coming out of his shell too.

'You're enjoying this aren't you?' she said to Killian, but he didn't answer.

'Well. What now?' Brad asked still looking a little vulnerable, which Killian thought was ironic as he was a poltergeist and powerful.

'It's time you went home,' Killian said seriously. 'I can send you there. Oh, while I remember — where is all the stolen property kept? I need to sort that once you're gone.'

'Why?' Brad asked. 'Are you going to be the one selling it now?'

'Nope,' Killian said with a shake of his head. 'I'm one of the good guys remember. Do you still not trust me?' It all has to go back to its various owners,' Killian explained. 'This is a police matter and I work cases for the police. You are actually one of my cases. That's how I found you in the first place,' Killian continued, telling him the full story. 'The thefts were being reported and the authorities couldn't figure out how it was taking place. That's why they hired me. 'They don't have the time to sort through petty theft, so the chief inspector simply looked in his local paper — saw me and that was that,' Killian concluded.

Brad thought for a second and then realised he was being hasty. 'It's all stashed over here,' Brad said and led Killian and Cleo to the lump of hessian that was piled up in a corner. Killian pulled back the sacking. It was like revealing the crown jewels.

'Wow,' Cleo exclaimed, 'how long have you been doing this?'

'A while now,' he answered. 'Not quite sure when I came here, time isn't something a poltergeist needs to know.'

'Wow indeed,' Killian agreed. 'I was expecting something along these lines, but not as much as this.'

'Killjoy hasn't been back for a while. He lets it accumulate and then drops by when there's enough to send to his fence, whoever that is,' Brad confirmed.

'That is one serious stash of goods,' Cleo gasped. There was an array of jewellery, watches, mobile phones, wallets, purses, perfume, cash and headphones.

'Boy, you've been busy,' Killian remarked. 'This is all going to take some time to process and work out who it belongs to. I'll get my girlfriend to sort it later with her boss,' the wizard continued and scratched his head.

'So you have a girlfriend?' Brad countered.

'Yeah. I'm not bisexual,' he added with a grin. Killian also noticed that there was a fair few different varieties of drugs too. 'I'm not touching any of this. Once the police know they can come and pick it up,' Killian said sensibly.

'That is just half of what Killjoy has already taken,' Brad admitted. 'I've been doing runs for weeks. I hate that guy.'

'What did you get out of it?' Cleo asked.

'My life, I suppose,' he responded.

'Well, you don't have to worry about him any more. And this isn't your problem any more either, Brad. Those days are truly gone, my friend.' Killian could see the joy returning to the kids face. He looked relieved.

'I-I don't have to do this any more?' he gushed and smiled and this was all Killian needed.

'Nope. It's time for you to go,' Killian said. 'Are you ready?' Brad nodded in reply. 'Before you go, would you mind telling me something?'

'What is it?'

'How did you die so young? You don't have to, of course,' Killian added, 'I'm just curious to know.'

'Killian. That's rather a personal question, don't you think?' Cleo cut in and sharply, peered into his eyes.

'No, that's all right. It's fine,' Brad thought about it and decided to tell Killian and Cleo exactly what had happened. It was the first time he'd told anybody — dead or alive. 'It was on a station platform, like this one.' He pointed towards the station. 'I mixed with the wrong crowd and they made me do all that stuff we're not supposed to do. Problem was, there was a rival gang and one of them caught me on their patch. It was a winter's night, just before Christmas. I didn't see him coming and he stabbed me and pushed me off the platform.' Brad stared into space as he recollected the memory. 'I don't remember anything after that.'

'Jesus, that is terrible,' Killian sighed. 'I'm sorry, mate. You shouldn't have had to go through that. You had your whole life ahead of you.'

'It would have happened sooner or later,' Brad confessed. 'I was doing bad stuff and that only ends badly, whichever way you look at it. I can see that now, but it is what it is.'

'I'm sorry, Brad. This should never have happened to you. You're a brave kid. But things will get better for you now,' Cleo sympathised, as she remembered something that had happened to one of her friends.

'Time to go, Brad, and leave all this bad stuff behind,' Killian said as he lifted out his wand.

'What do I do?' the boy asked.

'You don't have to do anything, Brad. Just go with it,' Killian said. He recited a spell, and with his wand in hand, rotated it in a circular motion, which soon created a revolving ring of light. The beam dazzled and hung in mid-air as the inside of the railway car lit up. The circle engulfed itself in sparkling array of supernatural matter. Brad didn't feel scared any more. For the first time in an age, he felt warmth and peace. The light lit up his face and for a split second it showed him the way he used to be before he lost his life. Killian was busy orchestrating the spell, but Cleo had glistening eyes and tears freely falling.

'It's pulling me to it, Killian.' Brad said, as a bright smile engulfed his otherwise trouble face. 'Shall I go?'

'Yes, you should go. Don't resist, just take your time and let it happen,' Killian instructed. 'It'll be fine, honestly,' he said, nodding.

'And Drake Killjoy can't get to me in there?' Brad asked, still not convinced.

'Believe me, Brad, nothing can touch you once you've crossed over. Evil stays where evil is. Goodness is protected forever,' Killian explained and the boy could see how truly honest the wizard was. 'There isn't a place more powerful than the afterlife.'

'I'll say goodbye then,' he said, but not before wrapping his arms around Killian's shoulders, before he stepped inside the ring. The sorcerer could actually feel his touch. It was the most amazing experience he would ever encounter. Cleo had to choke back her tears and turn away. Killian was having trouble with the huge lump he felt in his throat.

Finally, Brad didn't hold back any longer and released his grip and walked straight into the vortex. He was gone in an instant and so too was the void. It disappeared just as quickly and so did the light with it. The carriage was returned to its semi-darkness. All went weird and quiet.

'He's safe now,' Killian managed to say. 'You can look now, Cleo.'

'Shut up,' she retorted and gave Killian a playful punch to his arm. He looked into her eyes; she was more than just beautiful in that setting — she was positively angelic. Cleo stared at him and there was a momentary glance that spoke volumes.

'Got to you, huh?' Killian said with a grin, changing the mood. 'Girls,' he said mockingly.

'Oh, and what's that running down your face?' Cleo pointed out. 'Sweat, I suppose.'

'Nothing. Well, it is stifling in here.' Killian responded quickly by rubbing his cheek and grimaced because he'd been found out, when there was nothing there. 'Funny,' he reacted. 'I'll have to take you for a drink to thank you for all you've done.'

'You've got a girlfriend and I'm a lesbian,' Cleo reminded him sharply.

'A drink between colleagues, that's all. Don't flatter yourself, girlie,' Killian laughed.

'I've got to go,' Cleo said.

'Mmm. Me too,' Killian agreed. They stepped off the tram and went their separate ways. 'See ya, Cleo.' She didn't turn around, only lifting her arm to wave. Killian went back to the car park and secretly got his bike. When he got back to his office there were a few answerphone messages on his office phone. He returned the call.

'Hi, Penny,' Killian spoke softly into the receiver.

'Hi, honey, are you okay?' she answered.

'Yeah, I'm fine. Pickpocketing case is solved,' he told her. 'It took some doing, but all sorted. Can you sort the cash?'

'Wow, that was quick,' she said. 'Yeah, I'll have it put straight into your account.'

'Could you have one of your cops collect the stolen goods from the railway yard?' Killian gave her the details of the dry goods car.

'Yes, no problem, I'll send one right away. Do you fancy a drink tonight? We haven't been out in ages,' she asked.

'Why not? See you at the Square Inn at seven?' he said before putting the receiver down.

'Wouldn't miss it. Love you. Are you sure you're okay, Killian?' Penny probed with concern.

'Honestly, I'm fine,' he said.

'Love you, see you tonight,' she said and clicked off her end.

'Love you too,' Killian responded as the connection shut off. He thought of Brad for a moment, and then Cleo. He took a deep breath and made himself a coffee and slouched down on the sofa. He was aching more than he was before he went out.

'I'd better clean myself up for Penny tonight. She's gonna want to know everything about this case and my bruised eye. Oh, the bruised eye,' he shuddered. So, he finished his coffee and took a long, hot shower and let the steam do its work. Later he grabbed some painkillers before he headed for the pub and his date with Penny at seven.

# Chapter 20
## Spill the Beans

Penny was waiting for Killian inside, at the bar of the Square Inn. As soon as she saw his darkened eye she fluttered around him like a mother hen.

'What the hell happened to you? My God, that looks sore.' Penny said and winced for him.

'I'm fine honestly, don't fuss. You're not going to believe me when I tell you,' Killian said, 'but let's have a drink first,' he said, 'I'm thirsty and hungry. The story can wait.' He hated to explain things on an empty stomach.

'We're over there,' she said and he saw the table with a glass of wine and his favourite Cambrian beer sitting there.

'You're amazing. Have you ordered?' he asked. She knew what he liked — fish and chips.

'Yes… fish and chips,' she relented with a sigh.

'You're a diamond,' he said.

'Yes, I know,' she blinked. 'They'll be along with our food in about ten minutes,' she said and continued, 'I've missed you.'

'I've missed me too,' he joked and she gave him her strained look. 'I've really missed you too, you know. You look fantastic, you know that?' he added and her nose wrinkled as she smiled, which always gave away the fact that she was embarrassed but appreciative.

He looked at her and as always was blown away by her beauty. She was amazing. To say he was punching above his weight was an understatement. Any guy would give up everything for this lady. He loved the way her black hair hung loosely over her smooth shoulders and perfectly framed her pretty face. Her blue eyes sparkled from the reflection of the polished brass of the bar. She was wearing a yellow, thin-strapped top, which dipped in a V and revealed a deep, voluptuous cleavage. She normally wore a print summer dress, but tonight it was a denim mini-skirt, which showed off her long, slim, glossy legs. She was thirty-five but looked like a woman in her mid-twenties. She leant forward and they touched lips in a peck, and she stroked his arm affectionately. But he broke away because he felt a bit awkward, especially at the bar with all the punters there.

'Let's sit,' he said hastily and they made their way to the table. The pub was quite full and they didn't want to lose their seats. They sat and drank and chatted idle banter until the food arrived. Killian was ravenous and Penny looked on in amusement as he wolfed it down.

After dinner, Killian got down to business and went over all the events of the previous few days. It was hard for her to hear some of it and he could see her wince now and then. He didn't leave anything out — she knew what was involved in his line of work. She'd been caught up in one of his supernatural cases and ever since then, didn't question him on the subject.

'All Hathaway needs to know is that the thief is gone and the case is solved,' Killian explained, 'and the culprit won't be coming back.'

'I know that he doesn't want to know anything else anyway. He's happy as long as it is all sorted and he can wipe it off his records,' Penny agreed.

'Okay. Let's stop talking shop.' Killian looked into her eyes. 'I've had enough of work for a while.'

'What would you rather do?' she asked. 'We could go back to your place,' she said with a cheeky grin.

'Sounds good to me,' Killian agreed and returned the smile with interest. It was a fine summer evening with a slight cool breeze as they walked hand in hand. It didn't take them long to get to Killian's apartment. They were soon at the top of the flight of stairs and made it to his flat. As they entered his apartment, they were tearing each other's clothes off like teenagers. He didn't even have time to switch on the light as they awkwardly moved to the bedroom in a tight embrace.

Killian slipped her top over her head and she tugged at his shirt. She was soon popping the studs of his jeans as he pulled down her denim skirt. They fell onto the bed and rolled around in a playful, sexually charged, wrestling match. They devoured each other until Penny stopped when she saw his battered body.

'God, you've got more dark, bruising than white skin, Killian,' she panted breathlessly.

'Penny,' Killian said softly.

'Yes, darling,' she replied in a whisper.

'Be gentle with me,' he said with a giggle.

'Shut up, you idiot,' she said and they tangled in another passionate embrace. They kissed and caressed without saying a word. Finally, Penny gently pushed at his shoulder and he slumped onto his back. She spread her legs and climbed on top of him and gently straddled his slim body. She bucked and writhed in a frenzy of whimpers and sighs until they reached the pinnacle of sexual pleasure. Soon afterwards they collapsed in an exhausted heap, and finally cuddled until they fell asleep in each other's arms.

The next morning as the sun began to rise and a dim light filtered into the living room, Killian woke up. The room had a musky odour of stale wine and day-old perfume. He leaned over and gazed at his girlfriend as she slept. Her hair — perfect the night before — was now tangled over her face, but she still looked beautiful. He lay there a while and finally got out of bed and made his way to the bathroom. When he'd finished he washed his hands and gazed in the mirror. His eye was more yellow than black and the mark on his mouth had disappeared completely. He walked into the kitchen and opened the fridge — the cold air felt amazing as it pooled around his legs. He grabbed a bottle of water and snapped open the cap. He took a couple of gulps and as he dropped his gaze saw the folder Penny had dropped there the day before. It was sitting there on the coffee table.

So, he slumped down on the sofa in a giant groan. The feel of the cool material on his back was relief in the early morning heat. He grabbed the file and flicked it open. He read the first part of the document and was already immersed.

'Mmmmm. This looks interesting,' he said as he took another sip from the bottle. 'So this will be my next case…'

## THE END